LETHAL JOURNEY

Kim Cresswell

KC PUBLISHING

Lethal Journey/Kim Cresswell - 1st Edition
ISBN 978-0-9920841-0-3

Cover design by KC Book Cover Design © 2019

Visit www.kimcresswell.ca and subscribe to Kim's Quarterly Newsletter. Keep up-to-date on exclusive content, upcoming releases, first-to-see book covers, contests, and more!

For Justin, Carla, Porter, and Peyton

In memory of Mary Beech
Death leaves a heartache no one can heal, love leaves a
memory no one can steal. — From a headstone in Ireland

ABOUT THE AUTHOR

Kim Cresswell resides in Ontario, Canada and is the award-winning author of the action-packed WHITNEY STEEL series.

Her debut romantic thriller, *Reflection* (A Whitney Steel Novel - Book One) has won numerous awards: RomCon®'s 2014 Readers' Crown Finalist (Romantic Suspense), InD'tale Magazine 2014 Rone Award Finalist (Suspense/Thriller), UP Authors Fiction Challenge Winner, Silicon Valley's Romance Writers of America (RWA) "Gotcha!" Romantic Suspense Winner, and an Honorable Mention in Calgary's (RWA) The Writer's Voice Contest.

Kim signed a 3-book German translation deal with Luzifer Verlag for the first three books in the Whitney Steel series: *Reflection, Retribution,* and *Resurrect.* The popular series will be published in German beginning in 2019.

The Assassin Chronicles TV series, based on Kim's upcoming 4-book paranormal/supernatural thriller series: *Deadly Shadow, Invisible Truth, Assassin's Prophecy,* and *Vision of Fire* was in development with Council Tree Productions.

Web Site: www.kimcresswell.ca

Facebook: www.facebook.com/KimCresswellBooks

Twitter: http://twitter.com/kimcresswell

ALSO BY KIM CRESSWELL

The Whitney Steel Series
Reflection (Book One)
Retribution (Book Two)
Resurrect Book Three)

The Assassin Chronicles Series
Deadly Shadow (Book One)

The Sum of all Tears Series
Icehaven (Book One)
Liberty (Book Two)

The Raina Storm Thriller Series
Dawn of the Storm (Book One)
Dawn of the Enemy (Book Two)

Single Title Novellas
Lethal Journey

True Crime Quickies Short Stories
Real Life Evil
Murder on Sunset Strip
Garden of Bones
Edge of Madness

Chameleon
Backwoods Murder

**True Crime Anthologies Published
by Grinning Man Press**
Serial Killer Quarterly "21st Century Psychos"
Serial Killer Quarterly "Partners in Pain"
Serial Killer Quarterly "Unsolved in North America"
Serial Killer Quarterly "Cruel Britannia"
Serial Killer Quarterly "They Almost Got Away"
Serial Killer Quarterly "Lostmord: Murder
in German"

PRAISE FOR LETHAL JOURNEY

"An entertaining and complex novella with some solid twists at the end."
Cheryl Kaye Tardif, international bestselling author of SUBMERGED

"Chocked full of action. Lethal Journey fits the adage, "good things come in small packages".
Manic Readers

"A good read that rivals any police series on TV."
Me, You & Books

"Be prepared for a surprise ending that will blow you away."
Fran Orenstein, Sunwriter

"The cops. The mob. The district attorney. Lethal Journey is an intricate and suspenseful thriller that offers an action packed thrill-ride with stunning revelations and a nail-biting conclusion!"
Patricia, Room With Books

"Be sure to put this on your 'to-read' list."
Sharon's Book Nook

CHAPTER ONE

September 1997

Rain pounded down.

Lauren Taylor squinted through the windshield. A backwash of water battered the glass. She flicked the wipers on high and tightened her hands around the steering wheel. With a quick glance in the rear-view mirror, she noticed headlights behind her. The vehicle appeared to speed up, fall back, and then speed up again.

Her muscles tensed. "That driver behind us seems to be in a big hurry."

Her father leaned forward in the seat and peered into the side mirror. "He's all over the road. Might be drunk or something."

"He's crazy driving like that in this weather. I'm letting him go by." She downshifted the Jaguar and steered onto the side of the road and rolled to a stop.

As the van raced by. A giant wave of water pelted the side of the car.

Her father watched out the window. "Christ, he's flying."

Taillights flickered and quickly faded ahead into the blackened night.

With a quick glimpse in the mirror, Lauren steered

the car back onto the road, her grip relaxed around the wheel. "That's better."

Her father repositioned himself in the leather seat and stretched his legs. "The Law Society's dinner is next week. You going?"

God, the dinner. She'd bought an expensive navy and white designer dress for the occasion and even toyed with the idea of having her hair cut into something more sophisticated and polished for a New York district attorney.

"I'll have to check my schedule."

"Not good enough. I want you there, Lauren. My chance to show you off. Do some bragging, big time."

She couldn't help but smile. "Okay, Dad. Okay."

"And don't forget to bring a date for protection. Don't want a bunch of drunken seedy lawyers groping you on the dance floor. And by the way, I heard Eric was back in town."

Her smile faded as she remembered the annual dinner years before. She'd never forgotten a single detail of that night—how Eric held her in his arms and how his mouth devoured her willing lips then pulled away and left her mouth burning for more...

"What else did you hear about him?" she blurted out.

"Not much. Can't even remember where I heard the news. Thought you didn't want to talk about Brennan?"

"I don't. I just wondered when he got back."

Her father's jaw tightened. "Don't know." His voice turned hard. "Just heard he's back."

At one point in their relationship, Eric begged her to come with him and start a new life in Florida. She didn't have the courage to leave her father and walk away from her job. Four years later, she was taking on the most important case of her career—prosecuting Gino Valdina, head of New York's crime family, just like her father had done a decade before. But this time would be different. Gino Valdina wasn't going to get away with murder.

The sky split, and lightning lit the wet road. Lauren eyed the exit sign to Hyde Park.

The whining squeal of an engine roared from behind.

Lauren glanced over her shoulder. "God, that van is back." She clicked on the turning signal and steered onto the off-ramp. Her eyes darted back to the side mirror.

Headlights swerved from side to side.

A shiver drove up her spine. She clutched the steering wheel.

"I'm calling the police." Her father grabbed his cell phone out of the glove box and turned it on. "Damn it. I can't get a signal."

"Keep trying."

The van's driver gunned the engine.

The grill came into view, massive and powerful.

Close. Too close.

Metal connected and scraped against the bumper.

The van shoved the Jaguar ahead on the road.

High-beams from the other lane blinded her.

Lauren blinked and turned her head.

The van rammed the back of the car. Metal popped as the back window disintegrated into the back seat.

The seat belt snapped across her shoulder. Her head slammed back on the head rest then forward. "Oh my God!"

The cell phone flew from her father's hand. "What the —"

"Dad!"

Like a slingshot, the Jaguar shot down the slick road.

Lauren slammed on the brakes.

The car slid a half circle and spun out of control. A massive tidal wave of water washed over the roof.

Her father clutched the dashboard with both hands. "The tree!"

She yanked the steering wheel hard to the left.

Wood splintered. Metal buckled, squealed and cracked. The air bag struck her body like a fist and smacked her head against the side window. She pushed at it, viciously. With every move, fiery pain shot through her face and down her neck. The sickening sweet stench of gasoline and smoke filled her nostrils. Her head clouded.

Lauren heard her own voice, pinched and muffled, cry out. "Dad!" until her words drifted into silence.

CHAPTER TWO

Earlier that day...

Buff Stud Looking For Slender Goddess.

Get Real. Lauren leaned forward in the leather chair, sipped her Chamomile tea, and searched the personal ads on the Heavenly Dates web site. From her previous visits, familiar faces cluttered the screen. Page after page she explored. Blue eyes the color of a bright summer morning stared back at her. She clutched her cup of tea with both hands and read.

Professional Race Car Driver Seeks Intelligent, Independent, Slender Woman. Thirty-three-year-old male, six-foot-one, one-hundred and eighty-five pounds, muscular. Enjoys white water rafting, traveling and skydiving.

Again, her gaze wandered over the man's youthful face and broad smile. She read the small print below the picture.

Not interested in marriage or children. Only a companion.

In other words, just sex. She slammed the cup down on the office desk, tea splashed across the Yankees sweatshirt she wore.

The chime of the grandfather clock from the living room forced her back to reality. She closed the laptop lid and ran to the bathroom to prepare for dinner at the Four Seasons with her father.

With ease, she twisted and tucked her long chestnut colored hair to create an elegant up-do. Rays of light reflected down from the Pueblo design fixture high above the oval mirror. Hidden within the antique makeup tray, she found her lip pencil and lined her lips. Next, she added her favorite shade of hot pink lipstick to enhance her fair skin. Midnight black mascara over her lashes and her makeup was complete.

After hunting through the walk-in closet, she pulled out a classic black dress she'd bought last week. Perched on the edge of the canopy bed she dressed, and then slipped on three-inch black heels, careful not to snag her stockings.

Six long chimes from the clock blared through the house.

Her gaze darted to the dresser. Dozens of perfume bottles, atomizers, and Victorian powder boxes covered the cherry wood top. She chose a fragrance, dabbed a little behind her ears, down her neck, and inside both wrists. A rich bouquet of roses, sweet powder, and lily of the valley surrounded her.

Lucy barked.

Lauren smoothed her dress over her hips and quickly checked herself in the mirror before heading into the hallway.

"It's okay, Lucy." At Lauren's words, the chubby dog stopped barking and sat.

Through the living room bay window, Lauren watched the black Jaguar pull in the driveway and park. Before her father had a chance to knock, she flung the door open and smiled at him. He was dressed in a charcoal gray suit and crisp white shirt. He carried a bouquet of long stem yellow roses.

"For me?" Lauren asked.

His eyes lit, and he handed her the flowers. "Happy birthday." He patted Lucy on the top of the head.

The dog wagged her tail and bounced up and down, determined to play.

"My favorite. Thanks." Lauren kissed his cheek. "Come on. I'll put these in some water."

As she leaned against the kitchen counter and unwrapped the flowers, her father stood in front of the oak French doors that led to the cobblestone patio. She left the roses on the counter and pushed open the patio doors.

Her gaze wandered over the lavish green lawns with gardens scattered throughout. "My pride and joy." Parasol lights lit the huge lawn, abundant spotlights illuminated the multi-hued gardens.

"Incredible. Did you add more roses? Those huge yellow ones over there?" He pointed to the oval garden on the left of the patio.

"Yeah. Sun Flares. They smell like licorice."

A grin crossed his lips. "Hey, remember your tenth birthday?"

Of course, she did. Every birthday since her brother Jamie died, her father made each birthday count. Grown up fancy dinners at ritzy restaurants, extravagant gala parties and trips around the world.

"How could I forget England? Stately homes, castles, and abbeys, wandering through the lush countryside and those impeccable gardens. That's where I got my inspiration. I'd love to go again."

Her father smiled. "Ever thought about getting into

the landscaping business?"

Lauren laughed. "No thanks. I'll stick to being a prosecutor like you."

A gust of hot humid air brushed against her face. To the west, dark storm clouds built over the city as muffled thunder rumbled through the thick night air.

"We're in for a good storm by the looks of it."

"I think you're right," her father said.

She patted him on the shoulder and walked back to the counter to cut the roses. "Take a look at the living room. I finally finished redecorating last weekend."

From the open concept kitchen, she watched him look around the room. Honey faux finished walls warmed the room and cherry wood floors glistened with polish. A mixture of antique and contemporary furniture upholstered in faded tapestries occupied the space.

"Wow. You've been a busy girl. Looks great."

"I got rid of those sage green walls." She arranged the flowers in the lead crystal vase and placed the vase on the kitchen table. "That damn green made the room look like a stick of rotten celery."

Her father smiled. "My talented daughter. District attorney, Harvard grad, no less. Gardener and now an interior decorator."

She studied him unnoticed in front of the stone fireplace with a photograph of Jamie in his hand. His body slumped forward against the mantel. Her heart skipped a beat. He lowered his head and cleared his throat then stroked the outline of Jamie's face.

Inner torment gnawed at her heart and her mother's voice blared through her head. *I hate you.* "Dad?"

He turned. "How long have you been standing there?"

"Not long."

"You know this is my favorite picture of the little guy. I see so much of your mother in Jamie, her fine blonde hair and round blue eyes.

Lauren shivered. Thank God, she didn't look anything like her mother.

"How can you still miss her? It's been over twenty-five years."

"I can't explain it. I just do."

"I certainly don't," Lauren snapped.

Her father drew a deep breath. "Put the past where it belongs, Lauren. Today's special. It's your birthday."

Her thirty-first birthday. A day of celebration. But memories and emptiness surrounded her. A void in her heart, an empty place at the dinner table. Everyday growing up she'd pray her mother would die of old age in Woodhills State Psychiatric Hospital. Lauren would never forget Jamie or the woman who killed him.

Lightning burst across the night sky. Wind whipped through the trees.

She pulled the French doors closed. "We'd better get going."

Lucy ran to the front door and sat at Lauren's feet.

"Sorry. You can't come with us. You be a good girl while I'm gone." Lauren pointed to the doggy bed.

Lucy barked once and went and laid down.

"Want to drive?"

"The Jag?"

"Sure, why not? It's your birthday."

She snatched the keys from his hand. "Ready?"

"Let's celebrate." The warmth of his smile echoed in his voice.

❋ ❋ ❋

An hour and a half later, Lauren's father escorted her through the towering front doors of the Four Seasons Restaurant. At the top of the stairs, she glanced around the room filled with the upscale crowd. Actors, wannabees and the wealthy. Some familiar and some not. Of all the restaurants in New York, this had always been her favorite. She loved the extravagant décor—walls covered with a fortune of fine art and decorated with hard-to-find collectibles. As she walked past the white marble pool the soothing sound of water engulfed the main dining room.

"Good evening," the waiter said. "Would you like to hear this evening's specials?" He quickly filled the crystal water glasses.

"No thanks. I think we're ready to order."

"Dad, I'll have my usual."

"Okay. Let's start with a bottle of Corton Pougets 1995."

"Excellent choice, sir."

"For our appetizer, we'll have the Scottish salmon roll and some Osetra caviar. Miss Taylor will have the Dover sole with lemon sauce. I'll have the filet mignon, rare, with grilled portabellas."

The waiter nodded. "Very well."

When the wine arrived, her father raised his glass in salute. "I propose a toast."

She raised her wine glass to meet his.

"Happy birthday to my beautiful daughter. You have brought me so much joy these past thirty-one years. Cheers."

"Cheers." While she sipped her wine, he pulled a burgundy box from his inside breast pocket and slid it across the table.

"What's this?" The look on his face reminded her of

how his eyes would beam bright with joy at her and Jamie when they opened their Christmas gifts. Intrigued, she popped open the box. Diamonds shimmered in the candlelight.

"Dad, it's gorgeous."

"A little something, I found on Fifth Avenue. Do you like it?"

Lauren smiled and clasped the white gold bracelet around her wrist. "Of course, I do. Thank you. It's beautiful." She started to nibble on a bread twist and noticed her father yawn. "Tough day?"

"Yeah. I spent most of the afternoon reading through my old files on Valdina."

"You should be the one taking him on again. You're still the Deputy District Attorney."

She never forgot the look of disappointment in her father's eyes when the decision came down ten years ago. Not guilty of murder. With lots of money tucked away and dozens of associates bought and paid for, Gino Valdina's "friends" gladly would take the fall for him. Anytime. At any cost. And had.

"You know that's not possible. The farther I stay away from the case the better. We don't want to give Ricardo Pinstronna any excuse to ask the judge for a mistrial. The guy is the true meaning of a slime-ball. He gives lawyers a bad name. Did you know he defended a dozen of Bonanno's crew in the eighties and won?"

"I didn't know that. Well, he's not going to get his client off this time. Valdina's claim that someone broke into his house while he was out of town and slaughtered his wife for revenge doesn't wash. I'm sure he has enemies, lots of them. Being the head of New York's oldest and most influential Cosa Nostra for over thirty years, no doubt there are people lined up waiting to take him out and anyone he's connected with. The evidence doesn't lie." Lauren paused and took a sip of her wine before continuing. "Gino killed Madelina in cold blood. She was fed up with his 'goomatta' and demanded fidelity in their marriage. When he refused to give up his long-term mistress, Madelina took matters into her own hands and filed for a divorce. Not something you do when you're married to the mob. When you're a Mafia wife you're "owned" for life. I'm confident the state will prove their case."

"And I'm confident my brilliant and beautiful daughter will nail the bastard's ass to the wall."

She hoped he was right. "We'll get him."

Her father leaned back in the chair. "Troy said he wouldn't be surprised if Pinstronna wants to make an eleventh-hour deal."

Troy Granger. Assistant District Attorney. An attractive playboy known throughout the state of New York. Even his name made Lauren's skin crawl. She detested the man and the feeling was mutual. To fuel the fire, even more, her best friend Amanda Richmond had become Troy's recent love conquest. The thought of Amanda and Troy vacationing in the Bahamas almost made Lauren sick.

Lauren put the linen napkin on her lap. "I couldn't care less what Troy thinks. He's not running this trial. There won't be any deals. It's all or nothing."

"That's my girl. You sound very much like your old man. Hey, look. Here comes our dinner."

"Great, I'm starved."

After the waiter put the salmon roll and caviar on the table, they dug in.

When their entrees were served, Lauren pushed the green beans to the side of her plate and took a bite of the sole. Across the room, a waitress snapped a picture of a young couple cuddled together in a booth. The man looked deep into the woman's eyes, and then seductively kissed the woman's cheek.

"Dating anyone these days?"

The fork slipped from between Lauren's fingers and fell to her plate with a clang but went unnoticed due to the festive hum of the restaurant. "What?"

"Dating anyone?"

She swallowed hard. "You know I haven't dated much since—"

"Eric?"

"Yes, since Eric. Do we have to discuss this tonight?"

"I'm just concerned. You don't seem to have much of a social life."

"Come on, you make me sound like a nun. I don't have much free time these days. I volunteer every Saturday at the Humane Society. The Women's Law Association meets every other Tuesday and my days are pretty full with this case."

"What about your evenings?"

"I've dated at least a dozen men and you know it." She gave him a tight smile and snapped her bread twist. "Let's drop it, Dad."

Lauren glanced across the table at the Picasso hanging on the wall. Eric had always hated that painting, said it looked like mashed up peas and carrots and insisted on sitting with his back to it.

She never thought he'd turn his back on her as well. A flash of anger surged through her. Lauren grabbed another bread twist. The knot in her stomach added to her frustration...a reminder of how lonely she really was.

CHAPTER THREE

Detective Eric Brennan sat at his usual table and sipped the night's beverage of choice—a cola. In Chunkers Bar and Grill bellowing, pointless chatter overpowered the '80s rock and roll band on stage.

The last week was a blur. Every waking hour he pounded the streets in search of his father's killer.

Eric knew every detail of the shooters face, but not the kid's name. He'd heard from one of his informant's, the kid was a young tough-guy looking to be made—a "cugine" ready to make his mark into New York's most influential crime network, the Valdina family. As part of his induction into the mob family, the asshole had already killed a low-life rival family member and Eric and his father were working the homicide case when they got a tip.

That steamy June evening had started like any typical bust. Within minutes after Eric and his father arrived at the warehouse, dozens of DEA agents secured the perimeter. Eric entered the warehouse first, his father followed. Amid the stench of mildew and dust, the first pop of an automatic echoed within the barren walls.

They were ambushed.

His father, a veteran with twenty-three years on the force never saw the shots coming. Eric threw his body against his father in hopes of shielding him. It was too late. Instead, Eric witnessed his father's face, the sickening whitish blue tint that came with death...

While Pete checked in with the precinct, Eric shifted in the chair. His left knee still burned where the bullet had grazed his leg. He rubbed the scar, a permanent reminder of a drug bust gone bad. Very bad.

"Hey, Brennan." Pete threw a twenty-dollar bill on the table and downed the last swallow of his beer. "Come on. I think we got a lead."

Outside on West 35th Street, a full moon peeked through the clouds. Jagged streaks of lightning ignited the sky as rain sprinkled against Eric's leather jacket. He lit a cigarette and leaned against his white pick-up truck parked in front of Chunkers.

Pete smirked. "Man, I thought you quit."

"I did." Eric took a drag and stared at Pete through a haze of smoke.

"Yeah, looks like it."

"I'll quit as soon as you shave off that red mop you call a moustache."

Pete smoothed his moustache. "What's wrong with it?"

"Looks like a broom."

His partner rolled his eyes.

The drizzle intensified and a draft brushed across Eric's chest. "Are you going to tell me? Or are we going to continue to discuss the hair above your lip in the pissing rain?"

"There's a large cocaine shipment coming into Brooklyn Self Storage around midnight. Word is Valdina's crew will be there."

Eric checked his watch. Eleven-thirty. "Let's move. I don't want to be late for the show." He flicked his cigarette to the pavement and jumped into the truck.

Adrenaline pumped through Eric's veins. His fingers tapped against the steering wheel as if they had a life of their own. Maybe this time he'd catch his father's killer.

While Pete flipped on a map light and scanned the details of the bust, Eric turned the corner onto Pearl Street.

Two police cars blocked the street across from the storage business. Sirens wailed, dome lights flashed. A swarm of DEA agents and local cops huddled in the wide driveway.

Pete sat up straight in the seat. "Looks like they went in early."

"Shit." Eric slammed his hand against the dashboard. He threw the truck in park and then jumped out.

Pete was two steps behind him.

An agent met Eric and held out his hand. "Good to see you. What's homicide doing down here?"

Eric shook the man's hand. "I'm looking for one of Valdina's boys. What did you get?"

"A hundred and thirty-six kilos of coke. Estimated street value—fourteen million dollars. Someone is going to be fuckin' pissed."

A haul like that would put a huge hole in Valdina's pocket and cause more tension within the family ranks. "I'd say so. That's a hell of a lot of coke off the streets. Good work." Eric shoved his hands into his jacket pockets. "Any arrests?"

"Sorry, man. Not even a rat in sight. They must have been tipped off."

This was the fourth time in the last two weeks. Someone was feeding Valdina's crew information, someone within the precinct. Eric needed to find who was leaking the information. He paced between his truck and the sidewalk, lit another cigarette and took a long drag. Now what?

Pete tapped him on the shoulder. "Hey, just got a call. Stephen Taylor and his daughter were run off the road."

What? Eric stood speechless for a moment. "Are they —?"

"Don't know. They were taken to University Trauma. But check this out."

Pete handed him a slip of paper.

Eric read the details. "Keep a close eye on prosecutor Stephen Taylor and the new district attorney. They might run into some problems." His stomach lurched again.

"Are you thinking what I am?" Pete asked.

"Yeah. Thursday's murder trial. They were deliberately run off the road."

For decades, acting boss, Gino Valdina led New York's crime family. He was a smooth-talking piece of crap who had manipulated his way out of trouble a dozen times in the past. Easy to do in a city where associates, cops, and judges were bought and paid for with drug money that lined the Valdina family's pockets.

Pete opened the passenger side door and got in.

Eric tossed the half-smoked cigarette to the ground and squashed the butt with his foot.

Inside the truck, a familiar rush burst through Eric's veins. If one of Valdina's soldiers was responsible for Lauren's accident, he wouldn't stop there. This may be the break he needed to help find his father's killer.

"Didn't you say you dated Taylor's daughter a few years back?" Pete rammed a piece of gum in his mouth and tossed the wrapper in the ashtray. "A brunette. A real looker."

Lauren's face flashed through Eric's mind. "Yeah. Too bad she was such a spoiled daddy's girl."

Four years had passed, and he wondered if Lauren had changed.

More than anything, Eric prayed she was alive.

❋ ❋ ❋

"You're in shock, Miss Taylor. Please stay still," a female instructed.

Lauren moaned and turned her head in the direction of the voice. Her temples throbbed. Lights glared overhead and flashed in the back of her eyes. She flinched. A sharp pain ripped up her neck.

Gloved hands touched her arms and her body drifted back on the bed. "There. Now just relax."

Where am I?

Dismal beige walls surrounded her. A crooked picture of irises blurred. The smell of antiseptic caught her nostrils and the room spun. A face warped and distorted, swirled and twisted above her.

"What—hospital?" Lauren squeezed her eyes shut.

"University Trauma Center. You've had an accident," the nurse said.

Lauren's throat tightened. Images spun through her mind. Light. Rain. Metal. A van...

"My father. Where's my father?"

"He's across the hall. He'll be fine."

Thank God.

Footsteps. Heavy footsteps.

"How's she doing?"

That voice, gentle and familiar, wove through Lauren's groggy mind. *Am I dreaming?* So much like Eric's. Not Eric, though. He'd left her years ago.

"Pretty battered up. A mild concussion and her wrist is sprained. They say she just clipped the tree in that fancy car. If it had been head-on, we'd have quite a different outcome."

"Glad to hear she's okay."

No, Lauren had never forgotten his voice. Now that voice, deep and rich, whirled around her. She opened her eyes.

His face blurred, and yet she felt the need to lift her arms toward the fuzzy outline.

Features bent and twisted, for a second became clear. Brown eyes stared down at her then faded away. "Eric?"

"In the flesh."

What was he doing here? As far as she knew he was still working homicide. Lauren grasped the bed-rails and tried to sit up. Fire shot through her body and she slumped back, defeated. Though her head throbbed, reflected light glimmered over his olive skin, his smile shone down on her.

Another strike of pain stabbed at her temples. "My head is killing me."

"I bet it is. I'm happy to see you're still in one piece. Christ, you could've been killed."

His words registered on her dizzied senses, the tone of his voice, edged with concern. He sat beside her and placed a cool cloth across her forehead. The tips of his fingers brushed against her cheek, gentle and caring.

His citrus and woodsy scent was familiar and made her feel safe. Lauren looked at him. His dark brown hair fell at the back of his neck a bit longer than she remembered. He looked great but tired. Odd how their paths crossed again. Fate? Maybe.

"You must have stopped drinking otherwise you wouldn't be here."

"Been sober for three and half years."

"I'm glad. I liked you when you were sober."

The hospital room door creaked open.

"Miss Taylor?"

Lauren yanked the blanket to her chest. "Yes?"

Eric touched her arm. "It's okay. He's with me."

An untrimmed moustache almost completely covered the man's thick top lip. He looked like he was right out of the seventies.

"I'm Pete Hallman. I need to ask you a few questions."

"Eric, will you stay with me?"

"Sure." He nodded to his partner.

Pete grabbed the metal chair from the corner of the room and sat beside the bed. He reached into his jacket and pulled out a pen and notebook. "Can you tell us what you remember? If you need to stop, just say so."

She drew a deep breath. "Dad came to my house around seven. We chatted for a while, and then we left for the Four Seasons for dinner."

"Did you notice if you were followed to the restaurant?"

"No."

Pete scribbled in his notebook. "Any idea what time you left the restaurant?"

God, her head was going to explode. She chewed back a sob. "I think—ten-thirty. I'm not sure."

Eric's brown eyes met hers. "It's okay, take your time. What happened next?"

"There was a van. He was driving too fast for the lousy road conditions. I decided to pull over and let the driver pass."

"Did he?" Pete asked.

"Yes. Then I pulled back onto the road and then the van came back."

Eric stood. "You sure it was the same van?"

"Positive. That's about the only thing I am sure about."

"Color of the van?"

"Blue. Maybe black. And larger than a minivan. Everything happened so fast and it was so dark." She glanced at Eric. Two deep lines of worry appeared across his forehead, feather-like wrinkles formed around his eyes. "There's more to this, isn't there?"

His eyebrows raised. "The precinct got a call about twenty minutes before the accident. The caller said to keep a close eye on prosecutor, Stephen Taylor, and the new district attorney. Said they might run into some problems."

She took a quick sharp breath. "Jesus. This has to do with the trial. I can feel it."

Eric looked at Pete, and then back to her.

Pete flipped the notebook shut. "You know what you're suggesting?"

"It's possible, right? At this point, Valdina has nothing to lose."

"Possible. But if the mob wants you dead, you're dead." Eric said.

"Well if they wanted to scare us, they sure as hell succeeded."

"It's not too often the mob sends out a warning. In any event, we haven't got any other leads at this point."

"I'll have Dad stay with me. He won't be happy, but I think it's better if we stick together."

"Good idea. We'll have an officer posted at your house." Pete pulled out a business card from his breast pocket and handed it to her. "If you think of anything else or need to get in touch with us, call, day or night." He stood and slid the notebook back into his jacket, and then left the room.

God, she was alone with Eric. The only sound was the air conditioner humming overhead. Talk about awkward. She'd forgotten how tall he was. He made her appear petite even though she was five-foot-eight, a good four inches shorter than him. Their eyes locked.

"God, I must look like hell." Lauren looked away.

"You do. You've got one nasty bruise on the side of your forehead. Looks like the one you got from the guy who tried to mug you in Central Park. Remember?"

"I do." She smiled. "How could I forget? You saved me. If you hadn't, we would never have met." *And here we are again.* She fiddled with the elastic bandage around her wrist. "I'm sorry about Duffy. He was quite the character."

Eric slipped his hands into his jeans pockets. "Yeah, he was. He was a good man. A good father."

Lauren noticed Eric's eyes gloss over with pain—the loss still too fresh. She touched his arm.

"We'll talk later. I'll check on your father before I leave. Try to get some rest." He patted her hand and then headed to the door.

"Eric, do you believe in fate?"

"I'm beginning to."

CHAPTER FOUR

Eric met up with Pete in the hallway.

"Hey, the captain called. He wants to see you in his office first thing in the morning."

"Just what I need." Eric leaned against the wall and shook his head. "Did he say what he wanted?"

"Nope. Bromstrom needs to get on someone's ass. Fortunately, he picks on you and not me."

"Lucky me."

Pete snickered.

Eric stared at his partner. "What's so funny?"

"I saw the way you were looking at Lauren. You still got the hots for her."

"Give me a break. I'm doing my job."

"Nice bedside manner."

"For God sakes." Eric waved his hand. "Don't you have something to do for ten minutes? I want to talk to Stephen alone."

"Yeah, I could use a cold drink. Whether you want to believe it or not, you're still hot for her." Pete rushed down the hallway and headed for the elevators.

Eric glanced at the tired blue walls bordered with worn white trim. Pete was right. His feelings for Lauren had not disappeared. Back when they had dated, his social drinking got out of hand and her spoiled princess routine grew old. Not a good mix. He really didn't think he'd see her again. He couldn't afford to allow his feeling to get in the way this time around—it wasn't going to happen. Finding his father's killer was a top priority.

"Excuse me, detective. You can see Mr. Taylor now," the nurse said.

"Good. Thanks."

The night's events reeled through Eric's mind and frustration dug deep into his throat. He glanced at his watch. Two fifteen in the morning and his gut ached from the watered-down coffee he'd picked up in the cafeteria. He strolled down the west wing and pushed open the door to Stephen's room.

The man's eyes widened. His eyebrows shot up. "Eric?" He shifted in the bed and smoothed the blankets around him. "What are you doing here?"

Eric sensed the dislike the man still had for him. *Some things never change.* Stephen never approved of his relationship with Lauren. He thought Lauren could do much better than a cop. He wanted much more for his princess.

"Come on, Stephen. You're a smart man. Someone runs you off the road two days before one of the biggest mob trials in New York's history. It's sure as hell, not a coincidence." Eric took a step closer to the bed and kept his hands buried in his pockets.

"That van wanted us off the road. Pure and simple. Like it was hunting us down."

Eric studied Stephen's face. The man hadn't aged much other than a couple new wrinkles around his eyes and a few extra gray hairs. He had the same strong features as Lauren; high cheekbones, full lips and a smile that could melt ice.

"Any unusual phone calls? Letters? I mean you prosecuted the bastard years ago."

"Nothing out of the ordinary but why are you involved?"

Eric clenched both fists, his muscles twitched in his arms. "One of Valdina's men killed my father."

Shock burst across Stephen's face. "Jesus, I didn't know." His voice trembled. "Sorry about your father. A real shame."

Hard to believe Stephen Taylor had softened over the years. Not the same tough guy who had offered Eric a hundred thousand dollars to pay for his sister's cancer treatments providing he got the hell out of Lauren's life. Of course, Eric didn't take the money. Instead picked up extra shifts whenever he could.

"Yeah, thanks."

"How's your sister?"

"Good. The cancer's been in remission for almost three years."

"That really is good news. I assume you've seen my daughter—how is she?"

"Pretty groggy and worried about you. The accident could've been a lot worse."

"You're telling me. Not a ride I want to take again." The lines on Stephen's face finally relaxed. "Thank God, Lauren is okay."

Eric gestured at the white cast surrounding Stephen's foot. "How's the foot?"

"A minor break and sore as hell but keeping Lauren safe and making sure Valdina gets what he deserves are the only two things I care about."

"Guess we have a lot in common."

Stephen's mouth tightened a fraction.

Pete poked his head inside the door.

Perfect timing. Eric nodded to him. "My partner here

will get your statement. Can you think of anyone else who might want to hurt you or Lauren?"

Stephen pushed his head back into the pillow, his eyelids looked heavy. "No. Not a soul."

"I know I don't have to remind you to keep alert. You already know you're playing with the big boys. And these guys play to win—no matter the cost."

CHAPTER FIVE

Later that morning, armed with her father's overnight bag, Lauren opened the front door to her house. Lucy bounced up and down and whimpered with delight.

She bent and retrieved the mail from the foyer floor then gave the dog a long pat on the head. "I bet you missed me. Let's get you outside."

Her father hurried past Lauren, his crutches thumped and creaked against the hardwood floor. "I've got to make a phone call."

The scowl on his face said it all. He wasn't thrilled about staying with her but agreed they should stick together.

In the kitchen, she opened the French doors to the patio. Twenty-foot dogwoods swayed in the wind. Lucy sprinted outside, across the yard, and tried without success to catch a butterfly.

After Lauren changed out of the green scrubs the hospital had supplied and into a pair of shorts and a sweatshirt, she filled the tea kettle with water then made a pot of coffee. She eyed her father in the living room at the antique desk, talking on the phone.

"Troy, I need you on the next flight home. Sorry, I know it's a day early. Someone ran us off the road. Yeah, we're both okay." He paused for a moment. "Drop by after you get settled. No. I'm at Lauren's house." Her father was silent for a moment. "This was no accident. Yes. I'm sure. Troy—listen carefully. Make a few calls. See if you can find out anything." Her father hung up the phone.

She noticed his eyes—icy and unresponsive, his jaw clamped.

"Are you okay?"

"I need coffee." His mouth tightened more. "You know how I get when I don't get enough caffeine."

"I know. Downright ugly. The coffee is almost ready."

In the living room, she opened the drapes. The faint mountaintops of the Catskills came into view. Chickadees chirped and hung upside down in the trees along the driveway, just like her life, once quiet, now turned upside down.

She made a cup of peach-orange tea for herself then poured a cup of coffee and glanced through the mail. Like a kid at Christmas, she ripped open three of the dozens of envelopes.

"Take a look at these." She handed her father the vacation brochures and set his coffee on the desk.

He sipped his coffee and thumbed through each one. "Hmm, Abercrombie & Kent. Travcoa, Tauck. Heading to New Zealand?"

"Too busy right now. I'm thinking sometime in the new year. I'm going to need a holiday after this trial."

He flipped open the Abercrombie & Kent brochure. "Did I ever tell you I worked as a travel agent during my college days? Take my word on this one."

He handed the brochure back to her and gulped down his coffee.

"God, how can you drink that so quickly?"

"Practice, babygirl. Lots of practice."

"Want a refill?"

"Nope. Don't have time." He set the empty cup on the desk. "Got to get cleaned up and to the office. I want to dig through a few more of my files before the trial. See if I have anything else you can use."

Her eyes bolted to the grandfather clock. "It's early, not even eight. I'll drive you."

"It's okay. Stay here and rest your hand. I'll call a cab."

Ten minutes later he emerged from the spare bedroom dressed in track pants and a golf shirt. He looked down at the crutches. "I hate these damn things."

"I wish you didn't have to use them but doctor's orders. It's only for six weeks. You can do it."

Her hand ached wrapped in the elastic bandage. Visions of the accident played over in her mind. She didn't want him to leave but knew no one could change his mind, not even his own daughter. Lauren kept her thoughts to herself and chewed on her fingernails.

"Quite a surprise to see Eric."

"It was." She flicked an imaginary speck of dirt from her sweatshirt.

Eric Brennan. Tall, broad shouldered and handsome with a hot Irish temper. The thought made her cheeks flush.

"Hope you're not thinking about starting things up with him again?"

Lauren frowned. "Where did that come from?"

"I noticed that glow on your face when I mentioned his name."

"Dad, that glow, as you call it, is my happiness to be home. Twelve hours in that dingy hospital was more than enough."

A horn honked from the driveway.

"I have to go. We'll talk later. Make sure you lock the door."

"I will." When she held the door open for him she spotted the unmarked police car parked at the end of the driveway. At least she felt safe.

She touched his arm and managed a small smile. "Please be careful."

* * *

Amanda Richmond slipped on a body-clinging halter dress the color of lilacs. The deep purple shade enhanced her long blonde curls and dark tan.

"Looking hot." Troy slapped her on the ass as he walked by. "You won't believe this. Stephen just called."

She noticed a smirk on his face. "What did he want?"

"Check this out. He and the ice-queen were run off the road."

Amanda gasped and almost dropped one of the diamond earrings Troy had given her down the bathroom sink drain. "Are they okay?"

Troy rubbed his chin. "Yeah, yeah. Banged up. I'm sure they'll survive."

A glow of wicked pleasure flickered in his blue eyes and Amanda wondered if he had something to do with Lauren and Stephen's accident. Troy and Lauren never got along, even more so after Troy learned he would be 'second chair' in the trial, a decision made by Stephen.

"Do you think things will change after Stephen retires?"

"Baby, I know they will. No more 'second chair' for me. Lead prosecutor all the way."

Amanda smiled and wondered what he knew that she didn't. "Maybe I should call Lauren and make sure she's okay."

"Amanda, believe me. She's fine. Let's get to the casino and have some fun." He patted cologne on his neck and then ran his fingers through his hair. "You ready for the bad news?"

"What? Being run off the road isn't the bad news? There's more?"

He leaned against the bathroom counter. "Stephen ordered me back to New York. Sorry babe. Looks like our vacation just got cut short."

She rolled her eyes. "He orders you around like a dog."

"I know. But not for much longer. It's only one day early. We'll stay the night and grab an early flight."

"Damn him." She raised her hand ready to slam it down on the counter.

Troy caught her hand in mid-air and pulled her against him. "I love it when you get mad. That southern temper really makes me hard."

Amanda felt Troy's lips against her neck and her anger turned into desire.

CHAPTER SIX

Captain Bromstrom looked at the wall clock. "Brennan, you're here before eight. Did something happen overnight I don't know about?" He sat behind his desk shuffling through a tall stack of file folders.

"I thought I'd be on time. Besides, I heard you wanted to see me." Eric clenched an extra-large black coffee with both hands and leaned back in the chair. He stared at the thin, compact man behind the desk.

"I just wanted to touch base with you. You're still doing okay? You know with the drinking thing?"

He felt like a little kid being questioned by his father. "Look. You drag my ass in here every other day and we go through the same thing. No. I am not drinking. I am not going to drink. That part of my life is over."

"Just checking. I know you're under a lot of stress working your father's case. Hate like hell to see you suspended again. I had to pull in a lot of favours to get you back. You're one of the best cops I know."

Eric set his coffee down on the desk next to a photograph of Bromstrom's new wife, number three. He studied the woman with short blonde hair and round blue eyes. He realized everyone had a picture on their desk except for him. Some had wives or girlfriends. Others had kids or pets. What did he have? Nothing.

"You have nothing to worry about. You have my word."

"Good. I don't want to lose another detective." Bromstrom leaned forward in his chair. "I want you and Hallman to check this out." He tossed a folder across the desk. "See if there is anything in there that might help you get closer to Duffy's killer."

"Thanks." Eric scooped the overstuffed folder and gave the contents a quick scan.

"Remember the only reason I agreed to keep you on Duffy's case is that I trust your judgement. If you get out of hand, you'll be directing traffic on Broadway. Is that clear?"

Eric took a deep breath. "Perfectly."

"According to the surveillance reports, Valdina's been out of action laying low since his bail release."

"He shouldn't be out on bail, to begin with." Who the hell releases a Mafia boss on five million dollars bond? A judge bought and paid for by Valdina. Eric reached for his coffee.

"I couldn't agree more. But we aren't the courts. Anyway, word has it that Joseph DeSimino and the rest of the family aren't too happy about Madelina's death. The Organized Crime Unit says there's bedlam brewing within the ranks of the family over who should become acting boss if Valdina is found guilty." Bromstrom rubbed his forehead. "A Mafia hierarchy power struggle means only one thing. Dead bodies piling up on the streets of New York. Your father refused to wear his vest and look where it got him. Wear yours and watch your back."

"I will." With his coffee in one hand and the file folder stuffed under his arm, Eric stood and walked to the door.

"I want last night's report on my desk before your

shift ends."

"Yes, sir."

Eric made his way to his office past the room full of cops chatting back and forth and drinking coffee.

Pete sat behind his desk at the far end of the room. His fingers tapped against the computer keyboard.

Eric swatted a stack of papers off to the side of his desk in search of a spot for his coffee. "Twenty bucks to type my report."

"Sure. But you don't make any notes."

Eric laughed and pulled a crumpled twenty-dollar bill from his pocket. He folded the bill into a paper airplane and fired the money across the room where it landed right under Pete's nose.

"Thanks, man." Pete snatched the twenty and threw the money in his top desk drawer. "You seem a little giddy or something. You didn't get much sleep last night, did you?"

"Not as much as I would have liked." Eric didn't want to admit he was worried about Lauren. He settled himself in his chair and opened the file folder.

The shooter's face haunted him. A white male with long black hair and a large, jagged red scar above his left eye. It looked like some type of birthmark. Eric wanted to catch the bastard so badly. His pain was like razor-sharp claws, ripping at his heart, shredding away at him with a vengeance. Payback time? An eye for an eye?

No. He was a cop. Cops don't allow their feelings to get in the way of their judgement. Was he willing to give up everything to kill the man who shot his father? In a heartbeat. Judge, jury, and executioner. And that scared the hell out of him.

He took a deep breath and examined the black and

white photographs and names on the surveillance reports. Only three of the twelve were familiar. Giovanni
Spittasio, Christopher Valazza and Gerardo Bitondozzo,
all well-known top Valdina soldiers. Not the kid Eric was
looking for. If he could find out the guy's name—he'd
have his father's killer.

"Hey, did he give you hell?" Pete asked.

"Nope. Just his usual drinking speech."

Pete rubbed his hands together. "Sounds like fun."

"Yeah, a blast." Eric looked up to find Bromstrom
standing in the doorway. *Crap.* "Something wrong?"

"It's started. One of the patrols from the 76th found a
body behind the MovieCraze Video store on Atlantic Avenue. An anonymous caller said it was one of Valdina's
boys."

Eric leaped from the chair, grabbed his bullet proof
vest and jacket from the coat rack. "Today might be our
lucky day."

CHAPTER SEVEN

By eight-forty-five Eric arrived on Atlantic Avenue. Curious onlookers gathered and chatted back and forth, their whispers filled the morning air. Uniformed and plain clothed officers mulled about. The CSU measured the area while the crime scene photographer's camera flashed around an overloaded garbage dumpster.

Eric and Pete ducked under the yellow police tape. Like a dense fog, the smell of death and ripe trash coated the air.

The medical examiner was already barking orders. Simon Platts was not known for his jolly personality. Eric exchanged a quick hello and followed him to the body.

Cardboard boxes and trash surrounded a dented freezer. Stuffed inside was a man's body. A bloodstained blanket partially covered the corpse's face. A lone running shoe sat about a foot from the freezer.

"Interesting place to dump a body." Eric watched his partner's face turn the color of pea soup. "Are you going to survive?"

"Yeah, I think so." Pete covered his nose with his hand. "Man, I'll never get used to the stench."

"Anyone touch the body?" Eric asked one of the officers.

"Not that I know of." The officer pointed to a young woman at the back door of the video store. "She found him."

"Thanks." Eric then nodded to Pete. "See what you can find out."

Like a skilled surgeon, Platts slipped on a pair of latex gloves and snapped them around his wrists.

Eric forced a pair of gloves over his knuckles and swore under his breath. His heart pounded against his ribs.

Was this the guy who killed his father?

Like a performer, Platts removed the blanket.

Eric stared at the dead man's face. No birthmark. Shit. He turned away and kicked an empty oil can across the alley.

Heads turned.

With his fists clenched at his sides, he paced back and forth. After a few moments, he drew a deep breath and re-joined Platts.

"Having a bad day, Brennan?" Platts asked.

"Something like that."

A thin film covered the dead man's bulging eyes and his tongue hung to one side.

"What time was the body found?"

Eric stuffed his hands into his jeans pockets. "The call came in at five after eight."

The medical examiner nodded. "Judging by the body temp, I'd say he's been dead at least twenty-four hours." He bent down and examined the body. "Interesting. The ears are partially removed. And all these spots show distinct ecchymosis." He glanced up at Eric. "That's just a fancy name for bruises."

Eric knew what it meant. Typical Platts' condescending crap. He studied the numerous gashes across the dead man's face. "Look at the way those cuts angle down his chin. There's swelling and bruising around his neck. See, right there—just above where his throat was cut." He pointed to the shoe. "He was killed somewhere else and then dumped."

Platts turned the man's arm over. "Both arms and forearms have extensive and jagged knife wounds. Not deep cuts, slashes. Scratches and bruises around the wrists and upper arms. This guy put up one hell of a good fight."

Eric checked the man's pant pockets and found a worn brown wallet. He flipped the wallet open and searched the contents. "No money. No credit cards. Here we go. According to his driver's license, our boy is Paul Harvey Cassico." He placed the items in an evidence bag and sealed the bag.

Where had Eric heard that name before? Then it hit him. The surveillance reports Bromstrom had given him.

Eric turned to the burly officer beside him. "You'd better canvas the neighborhood. Someone had to have seen or heard something." The officer nodded and gave Eric a look as if to say, "Hey, whatever".

The medical examiner and his assistant wrapped the body in a white sheet and placed the corpse in a body bag.

"Seems like overkill for a mob hit. Any idea on the cause of death?" Eric asked Platts.

"Overkill for sure. Whoever did this had one hell of a beef with this guy." Platts zipped the body bag closed. "Hard to say all chopped up like that." He grabbed his black satchel from the ground. "I'll know more after the post-mortem." He turned to his assistant. "Come on, let's get a coffee."

"I'm done with Miss Wingard," Pete said.

"What did she say?"

Pete flipped open his notebook. "At approximately seven fifty this morning, she slipped out the back door to have a cigarette. At first, she didn't notice the freezer. She stated she thought she smelled something odd. On closer inspection, she realized there was a body and called 9-1-1."

Eric fumbled to peel the gloves from his hands.

Pete slapped the notebook closed. "So, who's our dead boy?"

"One of Valdina's less fortunate." Eric swallowed hard. "But not the guy I'm looking for. Literally another dead end."

* * *

Dressed in a white T-shirt and navy shorts, Lauren sat on the back lawn, pulling weeds from between the rose bushes even though she only had one good hand to work with. Birds joined in song around her. The rich dark earth felt cool between her fingers. She awkwardly pruned the stems and snipped a few dead leaves from the bush. Lucy dug her nose deep in the dirt and aimed to pluck a weed.

"Get out of there. You're not helping."

"Hello," a voice said.

Lauren glanced up.

Troy stood above her with a leather brief case in his hand and an arrogant look on his face. Wisps of hair curled against his partially unbuttoned shirt, his sandy blond hair was messed by the wind.

"Troy, you scared me."

"How's your hand?"

Lucy ran to him and stood by his leg.

Lauren smiled at Lucy. "My hand's okay."

"Here I'll help you up." He stepped toward her.

Lucy growled.

"Thanks anyway." In a lightning-fast motion, Lauren bounced to her feet and brushed the dirt from her hand. "Where's Amanda?"

"I dropped her off at her apartment. We just got back. She said she had some errands to do." He lowered his hand and tried to pet the dog. "Nice doggy."

Lucy snapped and showed her teeth.

Lauren scuffed the toe of her running shoe in the grass. "They say dogs are a good judge of character." Triumph flooded through her when his eyes narrowed at her words.

"Smart ass."

She turned and sat at the cast iron patio table. Troy followed with Lucy on his heels. He sank into a chair and ran his fingers through his hair. "I think you should step aside and let me take over the case."

Lauren laughed. "What? Are you crazy?"

"You're in too deep with the accident and all. Just thinking of you and Stephens' safety."

"What a laugh. Come on, Troy. You're not concerned about our safety. You're still pissed because you weren't offered 'lead chair'."

"I do have more experience than you."

"You do, but he's the Deputy District Attorney. It's his call."

His jaw tightened. "Things *will* change when the old man retires, Lauren. Don't think it won't."

The tone of his voice infuriated her. "My father believes I can win this case, whether you want to believe it or not. You, Troy, are only interested in cases that you think will make you look like a star. You're all about the glory and nothing more."

He snapped open his briefcase, pulled out a red file folder and shoved the folder across the table at her. "You need to sign these."

She shuffled through the papers and set them in front of her. "I support Dad's decision making *you* 'second chair'."

Troy slammed the lid of his briefcase closed, stood up and straightened his shirt. His eyes darkened.

Again, Lucy sprang to her feet and growled.

He looked at the dog, his upper lip curled.

Lauren leaned toward him and met his bitter gaze straight on. "You're angry that he didn't pick you. He must have a good reason. So, what did you do to piss him off?"

"I didn't do anything for Christ sakes. He's losing his marbles. You know—like getting senile."

Lauren jumped out of the chair. "I know my father better than anyone and he is not senile."

"You're—a—daddy's—girl," he snarled. "Face it, Lauren, you always will be. You really think you'd be where you are today without your father?"

"I'm damn good at what I do." Refusing to be put down by his vicious words she stiffened at the challenge. "Besides, where the hell would you be without my father?"

He didn't bother to answer the question. Typical. What in the name of God did Amanda see in him? Of all the men in the world, why Troy?

The muscles in his jaw tightened. He slammed his briefcase shut. "Take care of the old man."

"And you take good care of Amanda. If you hurt her, you'll be dealing with me."

He smirked and then turned and tromped across the

yard to the gate.

Lauren grinned. Maybe with a bit of luck, he'll step in some dog crap and get those expensive leather shoes all dirty.

* * *

After a hot shower and a cup of tea, Lauren chewed on a carrot stick and typed her password into the Heavenly Dates website. A banner ad flashed on the screen. *Tahiti anyone?* She leaned back in the chair and sighed. Turquoise lagoons, sandy white beaches, and dazzling coral reefs. She recalled her twenty-ninth birthday with Amanda at Club Med, in the Tahitian Islands. A two-week tropical fantasy, complete with free spirited bad boy types—bronzed and firm bodied. She sighed again. She was thirty-one, never married and men fell at her feet, but not the type she'd want to marry. If Eric's drinking hadn't gotten out of hand, she would have married him. Now she wondered if she'd ever see him again.

Her fingers glided across the keyboard and clicked on the button labeled, *Most Recent Ads*. She bit down on her lip and waited. Rows of new faces loaded on the screen.

"Lauren, where are you?"

Dad? She jumped from the chair and knocked the plate of carrots off the desk. "You're back." She snapped the laptop closed.

He made his way into the office. "Are you busy?"

"No, not at all. Just doing a little reading." She picked up the carrots from the floor and threw them back on the plate. She noticed dark shadows under his eyes. "You look tired."

"I am. These damn crutches are wearing me out."

"Did you get everything done at the office?"

"We're set for Thursday." She watched him sink into the soft leather sofa and rest his leg up on the edge of the coffee table.

"Troy stopped by. He needed some papers signed. He's not happy about being 'second chair'."

"He doesn't have to be. Not his decision."

What had happened between them? Her father and Troy had always gotten along and now something seemed to be wedged between them. "Did something happen between you and Troy? He does have more experience."

Her father put on his best poker face, but she could see right through him, the way his eyes narrowed slightly. "Like I told you before, you are best suited for this case. Are you questioning my decision now, too?"

"Of course not. I'm thrilled with your decision. I'll make you proud."

"I am proud, Lauren. You're my girl." He shifted on the couch and took a deep breath. "Well...I might as well tell you now. I've decided to put the house up for sale and move to the cabin when I retire."

"You're what?" Her childhood home in Poughkeepsie, her safe haven after Jamie's death. A place filled with so many good memories, not like the horrors she'd witnessed at the apartment in the city.

"I—I'm surprised. But, why?"

"I haven't used the cabin much in the last five years. I think some serious fishing is exactly what I'll need. Figured it was about time I did. I'm going to have lots of free time on my hands soon. I need to be doing something."

Now she knew something was wrong. Was he sick, or worse, dying?

"Don't give me that look, Lauren. No, I'm not crazy or

sick. I've worked my ass off and want to take it easy when I retire. Something wrong with that?"

"Not at all." She sat beside him on the couch and kept her hands clasped together on her lap.

A combination of sorrow and confusion plagued her thoughts. Life was changing too fast. She stared at the pictures on the wall behind the desk. A lifetime of memories. "Dad, I love you."

He got up from the couch and picked up his crutches. "Love you too. I think I'll go and rest this damn foot for a while."

When he left the room, sadness struck every bone in her body.

The doorbell rang. Lauren jumped.

"I'll get it," her father yelled.

She heard a male voice, hard, edged with control. Peeking around the corner she studied the man with her father. He was tall, his black suit simple, yet rich. Groomed to perfection his appearance commanded respect. When he turned Lauren saw his face and realized who he was.

Joseph DeSimino. Underboss of the Valdina family. What was he doing here?

He followed her father into the den. The door closed with a thud.

Curious, she tiptoed down the hallway and put her ear against the door.

"What do you want?" her father asked.

"Gino Valdina doesn't like the way your daughter is handling the case," the man stated.

Her father let out a raspy laugh. "I don't care what Valdina thinks and I doubt she does either."

"This trial will hurt her," the man said.

"Is this the only reason you're here?"

"She's playing with fire."

"Get the hell out, DeSimino!"

Footsteps shuffled across the floor.

Lauren held her breath and flattened her body against the wall.

The office door squeaked open.

"By the way, Stephen, your daughter sure looked pretty at the Four Seasons."

CHAPTER EIGHT

At the top of the winding driveway white pillars guarded Lauren's house like two comatose watchdogs. Eric stopped the truck and rolled down the window.

The officer assigned to guard the house poked his head through the truck window. "Your identification, sir?"

"Trying to be funny, Robson? Good thing you're a cop and not a comedian. Here." Eric handed the man a large coffee. "Figure you could use one. Did I miss anything?"

The officer flipped open the coffee lid and took a sip. "Joseph DeSimino stopped by, claimed he had an appointment with Stephen Taylor. I let him through."

"Isn't that interesting." Was Valdina's right-hand man hoping to make a deal on Gino's behalf? Eric didn't like the fact DeSimino was in Lauren's house. He didn't like it one bit.

The officer lit a cigarette and stepped back from the truck. "Pretty quiet otherwise. Not much traffic on this road."

"Let's hope it stays quiet and uneventful," Eric said. "Are you okay for a few more hours?"

"I am now. Thanks for the coffee, man"

"Anytime." Eric put the truck in gear and gave the officer a quick salute.

Next, to the house, he parked beside the gold Mercedes, shut off the truck and headed for the door. A covered veranda sprawled across the entire length of the home. He pressed the doorbell.

From the other side of the door, a dog barked. Seconds passed, and the door opened.

Lauren stood before him, looking sexy as hell, dressed in a tight white tank top and navy shorts. Her shiny dark hair hung in curves over her bare shoulders.

Eric shot her a smile. "Hi there."

"Eric. What are you doing here?"

Her voice sounded hoarse, frustrated. "Just wanted to check on you guys."

She looked past him to the driveway and pointed. "Isn't that why there's an officer out there?"

"Did I catch you at a bad time?"

She shook her head. "No, why?"

"You look stressed. Right there." His fingers brushed across her forehead. "You get a wrinkle above your left eye when you're upset."

"A wrinkle?" She placed one hand on her hip. "You're full of compliments."

"Lauren, I didn't mean it that way. It's a—cute wrinkle." He'd better change the conversation otherwise he wouldn't get in the door. "Listen, I need to talk to you about the accident. Can I come in?"

Her cheeks flushed a pale shade of pink. She stepped out of the doorway and let him through.

He walked inside and glanced around the foyer. "Really nice house. Must have cost a fortune."

Her full lips pressed tight together. "Oh, I get it," she said. "What was it you used to call me? A spoiled princess? I know what you're thinking. You're wrong. This is *my* house. I paid for it. Not my father."

Eric noted the bitterness in her voice, more like a heavy dose of sarcasm. He grinned at the fawn colored dog at his feet. "Cool dog. See she has wrinkles too."

"You're pushing it, Eric. This is Lucy. She's a Shar-Pei. I adopted her after Rocky passed away last winter." Lucy rolled on her back. "Odd. She must like you. God only knows why."

"Obviously she has taste, don't you?" He rubbed the dog's belly.

"Don't flatter yourself." Lauren spun and marched to the living room.

His eyes roamed over her slender thighs and legs. He wondered if she ever had the heart tattoo on her left hip removed. The dumbest thing she'd done in college—a game of dare, she'd said. God, she hated that thing. Not him—he thought the tattoo was sexy all the way.

Stephen was on the couch with a copy of the Pough-keepsie Journal in his hand.

Unwelcome silence filled the room.

Eric examined Stephen's swollen and discoloured toes. "So, how's the foot?"

"Pretty sore. Maybe I can get this piece of plaster off soon. Damn thing's heavy. I swear it's making my foot hurt more."

"Well I'm no doctor but I think you've got a few more weeks to go."

Stephen awkwardly swung his legs off the couch and sat up. "Well, if you don't mind, I've got a few—calls to make." He grabbed his crutches and glanced at Lauren. "If you need me, I'll be in your office."

After Stephen left, Eric sat in a chair across from Lauren and watched her trace small circles on the arm of the chair with her finger.

"Was it something I said?"

"He's tired, that's all. Now, what about the accident? Did you find the van?"

"Not yet. I need your help."

She bounced upright in the chair and let out a small laugh. "Detective Eric Brennan needs my help?"

"Come out with me."

"What? Like on a date?"

"Who said anything about a date? I want you to look at some vans. Maybe you'll recognize the make of van that ran you off the road." He watched her fiddle with her hair. A crimson blush ran over her cheeks. "You really thought I was asking you out?"

Why did she even think he was asking her out on a date? Stupid. Stupid. Stupid. What was wrong with her?

She swore her cheeks were now bright red with embarrassment. "No, I misunderstood what you were saying." She straightened her posture and crossed her ankles.

"You said you saw the van's grill so that's where we'll start."

"I doubt this will work, it was so dark."

He stood and put his hands in his pockets. "I know it's a long shot. It's worth a try."

"If you're going out, we need more coffee," her father yelled from down the hallway.

Obviously, Stephen had been listening to their conversation.

"Okay, Dad. I'll be back in a bit."

In the truck, Eric lowered the volume on the police radio. He felt her shudder beside him.

"Nervous?"

"A bit since the accident."

He glanced at her hands. "You clutch that purse any

harder your fingers will snap."

Lauren looked down at her white knuckles then quickly pulled the seat belt over her shoulder and fastened it. "I'll be glad when the trial is over. Joseph DeSimino came to the house and talked to my father. In a round-about-way, he suggested I drop the case. Eric, I'm really worried. Before he left he made it sound as if *he* was the one following us the night of the accident. He knew we were at the Four Seasons."

"What? Maybe Gino has DeSimino doing his dirty work now. According to mob rules, DeSimino is next in line if something happens to Gino. I'll have Pete look into it when I get back to the precinct." Eric started the truck and backed out of the driveway. "Try not to worry. We'll get this figured out."

On the way into town, she finally loosened the death grip she had on her purse and tried not to think about the accident, the images still vivid in her mind.

"How about we hit the store before we make a quick stop at the car lot? Any store in particular?"

She glanced out the window and pointed up the block. "McGregor's is fine."

Eric pulled around the corner and parked.

She got out of the truck and flung her purse over her shoulder. Stone walls lined the streets. Large baskets hung from lamp posts overflowed with multi-colored flowers.

Inside McGregor's, Lauren grabbed a shopping cart and made her way down each aisle. Veggies, fish, a couple steaks for her father, three pounds of coffee, microwave popcorn and a dozen other items.

"For someone who only needed coffee, you're doing pretty good."

She looked at the cart. "I didn't realize I needed so much."

Something about Eric's manner soothed her. Calm and reserved. Not tense and anxious, the way he used to be toward the end of their relationship.

At the checkout, the cashier rang through her order and Lauren noted how handsome Eric looked beside her, dressed in an oversized white shirt and blue jeans, his brown eyes sparkled. For a moment it almost felt like old times.

A teenage bag boy smiled at her. "Paper bags today, Miss Taylor?"

"Please, Roger." The young man packed two paper bags full. "Want me to carry these out for you?"

Eric picked up the bags. "I'll get them today."

After paying the cashier, Lauren pulled out a ten-dollar bill from her wallet and handed the money to Roger.

"Thanks, Miss Taylor," Roger said, his voice held a rasp of excitement.

Before the store's automatic doors opened, Eric turned to see the boy check out Lauren's ass. The pimpled-faced kid had good taste.

"I think young Roger has a crush on you."

Lauren laughed. "I doubt it. He's trying to save enough money to put himself through college next year."

"Good for him."

Around the corner, a woman sat on the wooden bench with a small boy by her side. Lauren stopped.

He looked so much like her brother, Jamie. He had the identical round blue eyes, blond hair, and button nose. The child peeked his head past his mother and stared at Lauren. Her mother's voice filled her head. *I hate you.* Her purse slid off her shoulder.

"Lauren?"

She felt Eric's hand on her arm.

"Hey, are you okay?"

Lauren swallowed hard. "I'm—fine." She blinked a couple times. In slow motion, she picked up her purse from the sidewalk and watched the mother and young boy disappear into a clothing store.

Eric held her hand. "What happened? Jesus, you look like you've seen a ghost."

Sweat prickled on her forehead and her heart pounding against her chest. "I'm okay. I think I'm just tired. I haven't slept much since the accident."

The child's face haunted her. What would her brother have looked like all grown up? Questions hammered at her, twenty-five years later, left unanswered.

"Well let's get you home." He loaded the bags into the back of the pickup truck.

Tires screeched.

Eric turned. The sun blinded him.

Gunshots pelted the back of the pickup truck like hailstones hitting a tin roof.

"Lauren, get down!" He ducked.

The large plate window in the drug store burst into pieces. Glass shattered to the sidewalk.

"Eric!"

He grabbed her arm and pulled her to the pavement. "Stay down."

She scrunched low, crouching and kept her head down. An angry crack filled her ears as a bullet whizzed past her shoulder and exploded into the base of a lamp post.

Crawling behind the truck, Eric pulled out his .38 from his holster and peeked around the corner of the bumper.

Tires smoked and squawked.

He bounced to his feet and fired a full clip into the van before it turned the corner and disappeared from view.

"Are you okay?"

"I—think so." Her voice was shaky, her face as white as a bleached sheet.

He grasped her hand and helped her to her feet. "You sure you're not hurt?"

"No, just scrapped up a bit. Eric, that—van."

"I know." When the smoke and dust cleared, he opened the truck door and sat her in the passenger seat then grabbed the radio. "Code eight. Shots fired. 440 Albany Post Road."

"Stand by...go ahead."

"Suspect is driving a black, GMC van. No plates, heading north on Water Tower Road."

"Copy," the female dispatcher said.

He dropped the radio onto the seat and put his arm around her. "It's okay. You're safe."

Lauren's bottom lip trembled. "Someone wants to kill me."

* * *

Lauren leaned against the wall and watched the desk sergeant chatting with another officer. Stale, stagnant air, perfume, and sweat engulfed the Midtown South Precinct. Fluorescent lights buzzed loudly from the ceiling and made her head pound.

First the accident, and now someone was taking potshots at her. Her stomach knotted. The more she thought about it, the more she believed it had to do with the trial and Gino Valdina. The latest attempt had her nerves on

high alert.

"Lauren?"

"Pete, did they find the van?"

He shook his head. "They're still looking."

She heard the disappointment in his voice. "Will Eric be much longer?"

"He's just finishing up with Captain Bromstrom." He put his hand on her elbow. "How about you sit over here?"

She brushed the remnants of crumbs from the chair seat before she sat.

"Can I get you some water, coffee?"

"Water, please."

"I'll be right back."

She glanced at her gold watch, a gift from her father on her twenty-fifth birthday. On closer inspection, she noticed a thin crack across the crystal face. The watch must have broken when Eric knocked her to the sidewalk. Thank, God he had. She didn't even want to think about what could have happened.

"Here you go."

"Thanks." She gulped down the water without taking a breath. "How long have you known Eric?"

"About two years now. Seems a lot longer though. He's a good cop just like his father." Pete looked at the floor and then at her. "Eric mentioned you two dated a while back."

"We did. That was a long time ago." Lauren swallowed the lump in her throat and decided it would be best to change the subject. "He must have been devastated over the death of his father."

Pete sat beside her. "He doesn't talk about it much. I probably shouldn't either. Can I get you more water?"

"No, thanks. I'm sure Duffy's death hit Eric and his sister hard. Knowing Duffy, he probably wanted a full Irish wake. He was quite the character, a real charmer. I heard on the news they were ambushed."

"Yeah. Eric threw himself in front of a bullet to try to save his father. Not many men would do that."

"Eric was shot?" She took a quick sharp breath. "I didn't know."

"That's why he limps sometimes. The bullet nailed him in the leg just above the knee. I think you'd better talk to him about this, not me."

"I guess I wasn't as subtle as I'd hoped. I'm sorry." When she looked up, Eric was staring at her.

"Are you two having a good old chit-chat?" Eric leaned against the wall with a thick file folder tucked under his arm and a tense look on his face.

Pete stood and slipped his hands into his pockets. "I was just saying the guys are still looking for the van."

"At least we know what we're looking for. A GMC Savana cargo van. For now, my truck is staying put. Evidence. Pete will give you a ride." He held his hand out to her. "Let's get you home."

She grasped Eric's hand and stood, realizing her legs were still a bit shaky. "Are you coming with us?"

"Yeah. Then Pete and I have a couple loose ends to tie up."

❈ ❈ ❈

Lauren unlocked the front door of her house.

"I saved what I could." Eric handed her what was left of the groceries. "You might have lost a pound of coffee and definitely the eggs."

I could have lost a lot more. My life. Staring at him for a long moment, she felt his warm breath against her face. Unaware of the world around them, their gazes locked. It was too easy to get lost in the way he looked at her. Each time Lauren looked at him, the stronger the pull.

She pressed her lips against his and kissed him. *What am I doing?* Her feelings evaporated, replaced with past hurt. She stepped back. "I shouldn't have done that."

"I'm glad you did." He ran his finger along her cheek.

"I just wanted to thank you. I don't know what I would have done without you today."

"I like the way you say thanks. Glad I could help. Try and get some rest—you look exhausted and a tad dirty."

She glanced at her white top smeared with dirt and noticed her nipples were hard. Why did he still excite her?

"I'd better get to work. I'll check in with you tomorrow." He turned to walk away.

"Eric?"

"Yeah."

"Please be careful."

"Always." He winked and then jumped into Pete's car.

With arms protesting the heaviness of the grocery bag, Lauren waited until the car's taillights disappeared through the white pine trees before going inside the house. She could still taste his lips on hers. What a stupid thing to do. She should never have kissed him.

Lucy was fast asleep in her doggy bed curled in a ball. Lauren peered into the living room. "Dad, you here?"

"In the kitchen." He dropped a half-eaten sandwich to the plate. "Christ, what happened?" He started to pull himself up.

"Just sit. I'm fine." She picked tiny fragments of gravel from her arms.

"The hell you are. Your knees are scraped and bleeding."

"Dad, please calm down." She sat at the table across from him. "Someone shot at me this afternoon."

"Shot? What are you talking about?"

"The same person who ran us off the road took some shots at me. Thank God they missed."

He shook his head. "Are you sure you're okay?"

"Filthy, sore and scratched up. I'll survive. If it wasn't for Eric, I wouldn't be here. Her eyes glossed with tears as shock set in. "He saved me. I was so scared."

"Babygirl, I'm glad he was with you. I'll have to thank him." He stared at his hands and remained silent for a long moment. A look she knew well.

"Okay, what are you thinking?"

"No one is going to get away with trying to hurt my daughter, no one. He slammed his fist on the table. "I'll get the son-of-a-bitch if it's the last thing I do. Maybe we should hire a bodyguard."

"You've got to be kidding."

"At least until the trial is over. Please think about it. I don't want to lose you."

"I'll think about it." Little did her father know, she wasn't about to do nothing.

She'd done that once in her life as she watched her brother tumble to his death.

CHAPTER NINE

The next morning, Lauren wiped her eyes, her vision still blurry, and read the note on the kitchen table.

Got a call. Went to the office. Back later.
Love Dad.

Even on crutches, there was no stopping her father. His dedication to the Valdina case was beyond words. Would he slow down when he retired? Probably not. It wasn't in his blood. She shook her head and proceeded to make a cup of tea.

Outside, sparrows dotted the edge of the birdbath, taking advantage of the brilliant early sun. She fiddled and stretched the ragged elastic bandage wrapped around her wrist. Once manicured nails revealed remnants of pink polish, chipped and peeled.

The hollow sound of gunshots echoed in her head replaced by an icy shiver creeping up her spine. The bold headline of *The New York Times* caught her attention.

The Countdown Begins; Gino Valdina - Guilty or Innocent?

Lucy let out a low-pitched howl.

"I guess you want to go for a walk?" The dog barked twice and sat by the door. Lauren swallowed the lump in her throat. She wasn't going to let anyone continue to instill the fear she'd felt yesterday. "Okay, at least let me get changed."

She put on a pair of black track pants and tank-top and white sweatshirt. After pulling her hair back into a ponytail, she slipped on a pair of running shoes.

Outside, Lucy ran ahead on the adjustable leash, leaves scattering under her feet. The dog high-tailed it toward the police officer guarding the house.

"Slow down girl." Lauren tugged the leash.

The officer shoved his head out the car window. "Mornin'. Great day."

"Good morning. It's a beauty." Lauren lowered her sunglasses.

Unruly dark curls covered the top of man's head. His chubby face broke into a wide smile. "Do you want me to follow you?"

"I'm just going up the road. We'll be fine. Seriously. Besides, I've got "killer" here to protect me. I promise I won't be long."

The office stared at the dog, and then to her. "Are you sure?"

"We'll be fine."

Along the paved road, tree branches creaked and echoed in the wind. Visions of the accident played through her mind. Every few minutes, she glanced over her shoulder expecting the worst. Not a vehicle in sight.

The Catskill's peaked and dipped into the fluffy clouds. Trees blazed with shades of crimson and golden foliage. The last time she had visited the mountains was with Eric. Tucked away deep within the forest, trout jumped from the stream yards from her father's cabin. The image of Eric's face dashed through her mind, the way his lips curled into a devilish smile when he spoke...

She wished she hadn't kissed him, but he'd saved her life. Even though the kiss was friendly, she knew her lips lingered too long, her heart wanting more. That would never be possible. If it didn't work the first time, it wouldn't the second time around. Lauren had been around the world, dated other men and never felt comfortable with anyone except for Eric.

During their relationship, she'd acted like the spoiled little rich girl he'd accused her of being. A woman who couldn't stand on her own two feet without her father. Years had passed, and she was different now. Wasn't she?

On the side of the road, Lucy came to an abrupt stop and growled.

Lauren tensed and grasped the leash tighter. "What is it, girl?"

Lucy snarled.

The hair on the back of Lauren's neck stirred. She spun around.

A black limo crawled toward them like a giant spider. She gave the leash a tug and quickened her pace.

The car continued to follow her.

"Come on girl, let's run." Before Lauren could get a good pace going, the limo drove ahead, swerved in front of her and slid to a stop and blocked the road.

The driver's door flung open. A monster of a man hopped out of the limo. His thighs were thicker than her waist.

Lauren bent down, picked up Lucy and held her tight.

The man grabbed her arm. "Get in."

"Get your hands off me!" Lauren jerked away from his hand.

He grabbed her again and shoved her into the back

seat of the limo then kicked the door shut with his foot.

Lauren cuddled Lucy. The click of the door locks sent a shudder down her spine.

She looked up and recognized the man sitting across from her. Valdina's lawyer. Richardo Pinstronna stared at her, his deep-set onyx eyes, hollow and lifeless.

"Sorry about my driver. He was a little rough with you. I figured if I asked you nicely to get in, you wouldn't."

"Damn right I wouldn't. Who the hell do you think you are? You think you can just scoop people up off the street. You know there's a police officer right outside my house?"

"Of course, Officer Robson. I've known his family for years."

Of course, you have. Why didn't that surprise her? Lauren realized the car was moving, rolling slowing ahead. "Where are you taking me?"

"For a little drive. I only want to speak with you, Miss Taylor."

"Ever heard of a phone?" she shot back.

"It's about the trial."

If he was thinking about making a deal for his client, it wasn't going to happen. "Take me home right this minute. There aren't going to be any deals. We've had this discussion before."

"It's important." He smiled benignly at her. "We really need to talk. Please." The muscles of his forearms twitched beneath his shirt. "I know you're very close to your father—"

"That's none of your business. Now, get to the point." She tried to see out the window, but the glass was heavily tinted, almost black.

Pinstronna crossed his legs. "It's been suggested it would be in everyone's best interest if this case went away."

She gulped hard. "You know that isn't going to happen. Take me home, right now."

"You don't have the evidence you need to convict my client. I'm just trying to be realistic. You don't want to be the laughing stock of New York just like your father was the last time, do you?"

"Your client is guilty, and you bloody-well know it."

The limo slowed.

He narrowed his eyes. "You know, life can change in an instant. Take for example your near-death experience yesterday. Life can be erased," he snapped his fingers. "Like that."

Her legs quivered. "Don't threaten me."

"Not a threat, Miss Taylor. Simply an observation. Gino Valdina's is dirtier than you think."

"What the hell does that mean?"

"He's has friends more influential than you or your father could ever imagine."

He tapped on the glass divider separating the driver. The car stopped and turned around.

Her stomach clenched, twisting to the point she wanted to vomit. "That doesn't answer my question."

The car came to a stop.

"You're a smart woman, Miss Taylor. This case will hurt you."

The passenger door opened.

"Remember what I said. And we never had this conversation."

❋ ❋ ❋

Standing in the middle of the road, Lauren's breath caught in her throat. Her legs were trembling from the inside out.

The limo vanished from sight.

Who the hell did Pinstronna think he was? How dare he threaten her? If she reported him to Judge Brookstein would she be in even more danger—the kind that could get her killed?

She raced home. Lucy dove across the kitchen floor and plunged her head into the water bowl. Before Lauren slumped to the chair, she locked the French door for the first time ever.

She snatched a bottle of water from the refrigerator and sat at the kitchen table trying to calm herself when the phone rang.

She jumped up and grabbed the portable hoping it was her father. "Hello?"

The line crackled and hissed on the other end.

"You have just won a one-year fitness package from Burgess Fitness Group," a female voice squealed.

Lauren slammed down the phone.

After a cup of tea and toast with peanut butter, she curled up on the tan leather loveseat in her office and scanned her notes for her opening statement.

She had to win this case. It was make or break time and her career was on the line. Apparently, so was her life. Her mind drifted back to what Pinstronna said in the limo.

Gino Valdina is dirtier than you think.

Lauren wished she knew what the heck he was talking about. An idle threat to convince her to drop the case? She couldn't drop the case even if she wanted to. Only her father could withdraw the case and that wasn't going to happen.

Again, the phone rang and broke her concentration.

This time she decided not to answer the call and waited for the answering machine to click on. When it did, she stared at the receiver and heard a familiar crackle.

Not again. She tossed the papers to the coffee table and waited.

A muffled voice said, "You're dead."

* * *

Eric sipped the black coffee he'd grabbed at a drive-through Starbucks and leaned back in the swivel chair. In the squad room cobwebs dangled from the florescent lights and swayed back and forth in the air conditioning.

Less than an hour earlier, he stood inside the iron gates of the pristine grounds of Greenwood Cemetery, immersed in another time and place. His mother, Eleanor, clutched his arm as they walked the grounds and laid a fresh wreath at his father's grave. Forty years of marriage gone in a split second. In the morning light, her pale cheeks shimmered with tears and her hands trembled. With damp eyes, he tried to swallow the hard lump in his throat. *I'll get the bastard, Mom. I promise.*

"Man, you're here early again." Pete slipped his jacket over the back of a chair. "Trying to get in good with Bromstrom?"

Eric sipped his coffee and gawked at the vision before him. "I don't believe it—you shaved your moustache. You really do have an upper lip."

"Had to. Judy said she was tired of kissing a broom." Pete ran his fingers across his mouth. "What we do to keep women happy."

"Speaking of women, have you met the Bromstrom's new wife?"

"Nope. But I noticed the perma-grin on his face since they got married last month." Pete stood. "How's Lauren holding up?"

"As well as expected under the circumstances. I have a feeling there's more to come at least until the trial is over. Let's hope she stays alive long enough to see Valdina behind bars where he belongs."

Pete waggled his brows.

Enough was enough. "Don't even give me that look."

"Okay, okay. Man, you've got no sense of humor in the morning. On to business. Seems your truck was shot up by a .38 Smith and Wesson."

"Hmm. Not the mob's gun du jour." Eric gulped the last sip of his coffee and pitched the paper cup into the trash basket. "While I make a quick stop at the morgue, I need you to do some checking into Valdina's crew, all the top players. Then I'm going to have a chat with our buddy, Jimmy Flame." He tossed his leather jacket over his shoulder. "If anyone knows about any hits out on Lauren or Stephen, he will."

"Okay. You think one of Valdina's boys shot up your truck too?"

"I'm not sure. Anything is possible. But that's all we've got at the moment."

"Hey, before I forget, what time are you coming over for dinner on Saturday?"

"How's five?" Eric asked.

"Perfect. Why don't you ask Lauren to come too? I'm sure she could use a break."

"What? You're playing matchmaker now? I thought that was your wife's job." Actually, Eric liked the idea. He

could keep an eye on her, make sure she was safe.

"Judy's making lasagna. Your favorite. She always spoils you."

Eric laughed. "That's 'cause I'm not married to her."

* * *

Eric strolled the barren halls of the city morgue, known as the Body Club. He could almost hear Simon Platts tossing medical jargon over his shoulder as he merrily cracked "freezer guy's" head open like a melon. A sign on the wall read, "*Rejoice in death and teach those who live*". God, how many times had he read that damn sign? Far too many.

The medical examiner was dressed in a green gown and had appeared to have completed the autopsy on Paul Cassico.

Eric pushed the intercom. "What's the story, Doc?"

Watery eyes looked back through the transparent face shield. "Brennan. Nice that you could join me." He stripped the heavy gloves from his hands and nodded to his assistant beside him. "Asphyxiation. There was bleeding in the throat and a fractured hyoid bone. For you, Detective—that's the u-shaped bone at the back of the tongue. We're looking at the joys of manual strangulation."

"With all those wounds and gashes the poor bastard lived long enough to be strangled?"

"Yep. The guy was tortured. Probably for hours. Fourteen knife wounds. His throat was cut last. The killer wanted to make sure he was dead."

"Any idea on the weapon of choice?"

"A twelve-inch saw back blade. Razor sharp. Survival type knife. He was stabbed in the right lung so deep the wound severed his spinal cord."

Jesus. Eric shook his head. One less low-life off the streets but he couldn't help but wonder what Cassico had done to deserve such a hellish fate.

"The toxicology report will be ready in a few weeks. I'll fax the autopsy tomorrow. Anything else, Detective?"

"Nope. That's good for now. Thanks."

Outside Eric lit another cigarette, his hopes sank. They had no evidence to tie Valdina to the "freezer guy" and after three months, not a single solid lead on his father's killer. So far, Eric had failed.

He went to the side of his car and kicked the front tire. A good shot of rum would have tasted a lot better than the extra-large coffee he'd bought this morning. For the first time in months, Eric wanted a drink.

CHAPTER TEN

Amanda clenched the steering wheel. "For crying out loud, get out of the way. Move your damn car."

She'd give anything to still be lying on the sugary white beach, sipping a Mai Tai, and making love to Troy. Instead, she was back in Manhattan blinded by black tar glistening in the sun, rising steam and suicidal drivers.

The endless line of traffic stirred.

Two blocks ahead, the tinted glass and steel of the office tower came into view. She glanced toward the sidewalk. Stephen? It was. On crutches?

Amanda honked the horn.

He turned his head and smiled.

She pulled over to the curb and lowered the passenger window. "Troy said you were just banged up. He never mentioned you had a cast and crutches. My goodness."

"Ah, nothing to worry about." He ducked his head in the window. "Look at you. Nice tan. You must have had a good time."

Would have been better if we didn't have to be back a day early. She bit her tongue and forced a smile. "Absolutely delightful."

A horn honked from behind.

Her gaze shifted to the rear-view mirror. A black van slowed to a crawl. Like enormous jaws, the chrome grill neared, ready to consume her compact car. Clouds of exhaust billowed from the muffler in the cool morning air.

Stephen straightened and hobbled back a few steps from the car, his gaze glued to the van. "Probably wants to snag your parking spot." He continued to stare at the van.

Her eyes widened. "Is something wrong?"

"Amanda, I'll catch up with you later."

"Stephen—"

"Get going." He hesitated, then turned a lame smile to her. "Sorry. Didn't mean to snarl at you."

Amanda glanced back at the van. "Friend of yours?"

"Just someone I know. You'll be back to work tomorrow morning?"

"Bright eyed and bushy tailed. A law clerk's job is never done. I'm sure my desk is stacked sky high with work. I'll be busy as a stump-tailed cow in fly time."

Odd? He never cracked a grin. He always laughed at her southern sayings.

"Okay, see you then. Glad you're back." Stephen waved, and shooed her on.

Amanda put the car in drive and crept back into the traffic. From the side mirror, she watched him crutch his way over to the van's passenger door.

Her eyes drifted to the traffic ahead.

At the intersection, the light turned red.

She glanced over her shoulder.

The van was gone.

So was Stephen.

❊ ❊ ❊

Lauren pressed the rewind button on the answering machine, and then pushed play for the tenth time. She bit her nails and listened.

The voice was distorted, barely audible. She couldn't tell if the voice was male or female, but the message was clear.

Someone wanted her dead.

Valdina? His lawyer? Someone she'd convicted in the past? God, she didn't know what to think. A hurricane of nausea swirled in her stomach. Bent over with her head between her legs, she stared at the floor and took deep breaths until the queasiness subsided.

Eric. She needed to see him, now.

She grabbed the tape from the answering machine and tossed it in her purse. Out the living window, she looked at her Mercedes in the driveway. An uncontrollable rush of tremors shook her body. The muscles in her legs quivered. Clearly, she couldn't drive. She called a cab instead. The grandfather clock struck seven-thirty as she locked the front door.

❋ ❋ ❋

An hour and forty minutes later, Lauren arrived at the Midtown South Precinct. She tossed a handful of bills at the driver who snatched the money and blessed her with a toothless smile. The cab screeched away into the morning traffic as the blue sky turned a gloomy shade of gray.

The desk sergeant grinned. "You're back."

"I need to see Detective Brennan. It's crucial."

"Brennan's not in right now. He should be back soon."

Her heart sank.

"Hallman can see you in ten minutes."

"Okay. I'll wait."

"You can wait in there." The sergeant pointed to the small lobby crammed with people.

Lauren clutched her purse and leaned against the wall. Not an empty chair in the place. A woman with blazing mile-high spikes of blue hair dressed in a halter-top and a plastic mini-skirt winked at her. Lauren lowered her eyes to the stained blue carpet and grasped her purse tighter. Then she heard his voice.

"Eric?"

He turned. "Lauren, what are you doing here?"

"I need to talk to you." Her voice trembled. "Something has happened."

"Come on." He guided her to his office and closed the door. He sat on the edge of his desk. "What's going on?"

She opened her purse and handed him the tape.

"What's this?"

"A threat." She paced the room while he dug through a drawer and pulled out a mini-tape recorder.

While the tape played his eyes widened. "When did you get the call?"

"This morning after I took Lucy for a walk." Should she tell Eric everything? No, it might put her in more danger. "I'm scared. I've been run off the road, shot at, and now this. I don't know how much more I can take."

Eric moved in front of her and put his arm around her. "Everything will okay. We'll find who's doing this."

The warmth and strength of his arms calmed her, but only for a moment as a loud rap at the door broke the silence and their embrace.

Eric motioned to Pete.

"Am I interrupting?"

"No. We have a new problem." Eric played Lauren's message again and then tossed Pete the tape. "Can you take this down to the lab? We need it processed pronto. After that, I'd feel better if you were posted at Lauren's house instead of Robson. Keep your eyes open."

"I will," Pete said and grabbed the tape.

Eric looked at her. "I think we should check some of your recent cases."

"So you don't think this latest threat has to do with Valdina or the trial?"

He rubbed his left knee. "Honestly, I don't know. I think we need to keep an open mind and check all possibilities.

"Pete, I'll meet you at Lauren's in a few hours."

Before Pete left he stopped and touched Lauren's arm. "You have the best two detectives working on this." His eyes shifted to Eric. "Later, man."

Eric stood and grasped her hand. "We will find out who's doing this."

"Why is this happening? Is someone really out to get me? My father? Or both of us? It just doesn't make sense that Valdina would do this, not at this point. Sure he has a lot to lose if he's convicted—why risk everything days before the trial?"

"I wish I knew." He let go of her hand. "You up to working together?"

"Of course. Whatever it takes. What do you have in mind?"

"Where do you keep your files?" He grabbed his car keys off of his desk and shoved them in his jeans pocket.

"My upcoming cases, I have at home. The rest are at the office."

"Well let's start at your house and go from there. How about I'll pick you up out front in five minutes?"

"Okay." Lauren repositioned her purse on her shoulder and opened the office door.

On the way out of the precinct, an old man dressed in

dirty clothes staggered, his white hair looked like a bird's nest, tangled and matted. He stopped and pointed at her.

"I want that little cutie."

His legs wobbled. "She's so pretty." He let out a loud belch.

"Come on." An officer groaned and hauled the drunk past her. "Time to sleep it off. Sid."

The vile stench of whiskey surrounded her. Her breath came faster and faster then the world blurred. Her mother's voice shouted in her head.

Madison took a step toward her, and then a step back; her feet stumbled over the throw rug. "Keep your mouth shut Lauren or I'll beat the shit outta of you!"

She put a brown bottle to her mouth and took a big gulp like she was drinking a bottle of pop. "I gave up my acting career for this? I could'a been a star."

Her eyes shifted from Lauren to her little brother. "And you, you little bastard. Next time you'll eat what I put on your plate or you starve. Go to your room. Now!"

"Mommy, no!" Lauren tried to push her younger brother Jamie behind her, out of the way, but Mommy got to him anyway.

"Mommy, please! Leave him alone!" Lauren wailed. She watched her mother's eyes. They looked huge and mean. So scary. When mommy grabbed Jamie's arm, Lauren hid around the corner and whimpered.

Jamie tried to get away but couldn't. He twisted and kicked and then shut his eyes and yelled. "Mommy!"

Mommy closed her hand tight, clenched her teeth like a dog and hit Jamie on the back of his head. He bounced down the stairs like a ball. He didn't move and lots of blood came out of his mouth and made a mess on the floor.

Lauren stared down at him. She felt dizzy like she couldn't stand anymore. She shivered.

She needed Daddy.

She ran as fast as her legs could carry her into the spare bedroom and dialed the phone.

She heard his voice. "Stephen Taylor."

"Daddy, come home quick!" she cried into the phone.

"Lauren? What's wrong?"

"Mommy hurt Jamie...hurry, Daddy...hurry!"

"Honey, where's Jamie?"

"Downstairs. Jamie's hurt."

"Oh, my God! Where are you?

"In—in the extra room."

"Listen to me, honey. Lock the door, okay and stay there. I'll be right home."

"Miss? Miss? Are you okay?"

Lauren blinked. The desk sergeant's face slowly came into focus. "I'm—fine."

"Thought you were going to faint right here. Wanna sit?"

"I just need some air." She rushed to the front door and stepped outside.

A chilly breeze kicked through her hair and drizzle showered her face.

It was hard to believe that after twenty-five years her mother's voice still made her tremble with fear to the point of almost passing out.

* * *

In the warmth of Eric's car, Lauren rested her head on the headrest. Rows of houses sped by, rain streaked down the car's windows like slow-moving winding rivers. She fiddled with her hair. The silence between them during the drive back to her house made her uncomfortable.

"Didn't you have a pet name for this car?"

Eric smiled. "Still do. Ironride. For a '68, she's still in great shape. I don't have the heart to sell her."

"Men and their cars."

"Women and their shoes."

She kept her eyes lowered and rolled the car window down half way. A welcome breeze brushed against her face. "So, where you living now?"

"I bought a small condo, a Brownstone, over on 10th Street. I haven't had much time to decorate. Maybe you can drop by sometime. I could use some ideas. I'm really am sorry about Rocky. I know how much you loved that dog." His voice sounded shaky when he spoke.

"Yeah, I did—and if I remember right, so did you. I miss him a lot, but it's helped having Lucy around."

The tension between them seemed to melt away. Relaxed back in the seat she glanced at him, and then to his strong hands wrapped around the steering wheel. He always hated his hands, said they were too large. Lauren ignored the twinge in her heart. Even though she didn't want to admit it, she really had missed Eric. Missed his voice and missed his touch.

She jolted up in the seat and pointed to the ditch. "Stop Eric, that's my dog."

"What's she doing out here?"

"I don't know. Unless Dad let her out and she escaped the yard. She's never done that before."

Eric steered the car to the shoulder of the road and stopped.

Lauren opened the door and stared at Lucy, whimpering, soaking wet and covered with dirt. "Oh, you poor thing."

"I'll see if I've got something to wrap her in."

He covered the dog with a flannel shirt he had in the car and put her on Lauren's lap.

She coddled the dog in her arms. "We're almost home. A few more minutes."

The car crawled to a stop.

"What's wrong?"

"I don't see—" Eric opened the glove box, pulled out a gun and placed it on the dash. He put the car in drive.

Lauren held the dog tighter as they rolled their way to the brown Impala parked at the end of the driveway.

Eric threw the car in park and grabbed his gun. "Stay put."

She watched him make his way to the car with his gun pointed toward the ground.

The wind shifted, and the sky darkened. A crack of thunder pierced the air and shook the car.

She thought she'd heard Eric yelling but couldn't make out what he was saying. She rolled down the window and listened.

Another loud clap of thunder.

The hairs on the back of her neck stirred. *Something's wrong.* She left Lucy on the front seat and jumped out of the Mustang.

Lauren ran in Eric's direction. "What is it, Eric?"

She came to an abrupt stop.

A male body lay in the rain-soaked grass.

Eric stared up at Lauren with empty eyes, a look that paralysed her to silence.

CHAPTER ELEVEN

Eric rolled Pete onto his back. Blood spurted from his abdomen and formed a crimson stream beneath the unmarked car. Eric glanced at his own blood-stained fingers and memories flooded his mind.

In the warehouse between the stacks of crates, Eric slithered on his stomach in hopes of getting a better view.

A barrage of explosive pops surrounded him.

Like a tornado, dust and dirt swirled across the warehouse. Flashes of light...the clink of spent shells hitting the concrete floor...the smell of gun powder, the smell lingering everywhere...

Cold driving rain pelted Eric's face and brought him back to the present. This was his fault. If he hadn't told Pete to replace Robson...

"Lauren, give me your sweatshirt."

She ripped it off and handed it to him.

He placed it against the bullet hole then grabbed her hand. "Press here. Hard."

"I don't know if—"

"Lauren, do it. He'll die if you don't."

She dropped to her knees and pressed the shirt against the wound.

While Eric called 9-1-1, Pete made gurgling noises.

Thick blood trickled down the side of his mouth.

"Brennan." Pete gasped for a breath.

Eric got on his knees. "I'm here. Hang in there, buddy."

He grabbed for Eric's jacket. His fingers turned to claws and it took all his breath to spit out two words. "Black van."

"Okay. Stay quiet." Eric grabbed his partner's hand and held it tight.

Pete made more gurgling sounds. "Tell—"

"Don't talk. The ambulance will be here any minute."

"Tell Judy...I love..." His head fell to one side.

Eric yanked at Pete's hand. "Damn it, he's not breathing."

In the distance, sirens wailed.

Eric gulped hard. Rain soaked his face and blurred his vision.

Without hesitation, Lauren kept applying pressure to Pete's wound with one hand. She opened his mouth and pressed her lips against his mouth. With a deep breath, she blew hard while Eric watched his chest.

Nothing.

She tried again.

Eric started chest compressions the best he could. "Come on."

They continued to do CPR until the ambulance pulled into the driveway followed by three police cars.

"Come on, you can do this, I know you can." He continued to pump Pete's chest. "Breathe. God damn it!"

An EMT dropped to her knees and jerked open her medical kit and fumbled for a stethoscope. "How long has he been down?"

"A couple of minutes."

"Get out of the way. We'll take over from here," she

said in a calm stern voice.

Eric lunged to his feet. "Please help him. He's my part-ner."

The EMT glanced up at him. "We'll do everything we can."

The next five minutes seemed like hours. Eric helped the EMT personnel load the gurney into the back of the ambulance.

He slammed the ambulance door shut. "Where you taking him?"

"St. Francis. If we don't, he won't make it."

Tires sloshed in the mud and flashing lights lit in all directions. Eric squinted and scanned the tree line. Was the shooter lurking? Watching?

Lauren was dripping wet and looked like she was in shock. He wrapped a blanket around her shoulders. "I have to go. Sheriff Stanton is over there." Eric pointed to a group of Poughkeepsie police officers. "And this is Dep-uty Murphy. He'll look after you. You'll be safe."

Eric pushed her bangs to one side. "I've got to be with Pete."

"Eric—will he be okay?"

"I don't know. Pray Lauren. Pray hard."

❋ ❋ ❋

"My house!" Lauren stared at the living room unable to move. Jagged glass layered the floor and smashed an-tique furniture was heaved in discarded ruins.

Deputy Murphy's eyebrows shot up. "Stay right here." He pulled out his revolver and began to search the house.

With a slight movement of her shoe, glass crackled and crunched. She held Lucy and sat on the bench by the front door. For years, she'd searched to find the traditional furniture for her house, like the hand-carved walnut desk she'd bought in England. All destroyed. She wanted to cry.

Lucy let out a growl.

Lauren cringed at the hollow thump of footsteps coming from the hallway.

Deputy Murphy glanced around. "The place is clear."

"I need to change out of these wet clothes."

"Go ahead."

Lauren placed Lucy in her doggy bed and headed for the bathroom. She stopped in front of her office. Her vision widened. More destruction. She swallowed the lump in her throat and took one step in, and then another. Her beloved New York State Bar Association certificate hung to one side, the framed cracked, glass shattered. Dozens of books tossed from the ceiling high oak selves were scattered across the room. Her case files were shredded. She poked her head behind the office door at the curio cabinet with the doors torn from the hinges. The concentrated stench of spray paint lingered in the air and made her stomach roil.

Her father had wanted her to live in a more populated area of town. Now she understood why. With the closest neighbour a mile away, no one would've heard or seen anything.

In the bathroom, she tore the wet elastic bandage from her wrist and scrubbed her blood stained hands and face until her skin burned red with fire. After giving her hair a quick towel dry she changed into a navy tracksuit she'd left hanging behind the bathroom door and went back out into the living room.

"You might want to get a motel room for the night," Deputy Murphy said.

"No way. This is my house, and no one is running me out."

"Suit yourself."

Outside the world darkened, and wind howled and groaned. On the veranda, voices mumbled, footsteps pounded, closer and closer. The front door creaked open.

Sheriff Stanton stood with his hands in his jacket pocket. His chest heaved as he took a breath. The strong odour of cigarette smoke engulfed the foyer. "Get to work," he said to the crime scene technicians huddled in the doorway.

Her home filled with unfamiliar faces. Their voices invaded her thoughts and conversations turned into disjointed ramble. She pressed the heel of her hand to her forehead. Her mind whirled. Valdina had something to do with this and she'd find a way to prove it.

"Sheriff? Any news on Pete's condition?"

"Not yet. If I hear anything, I'll let you know."

"Thanks."

For the next two hours officers from the Duchess County Sheriff's Office and the Poughkeepsie Police Department paraded in and out, some in uniform, others dressed in jeans and jackets from the detective unit. Noise and chatter plagued her mind. With a long, fatigued sigh, she stood and stretched her legs. Her muscles squealed with strain.

"Miss Taylor." Deputy Murphy cocked his head around the corner of the hall. "The crime scene unit got some partial prints from the patio door lock where the intruder broke in. A slim chance, but maybe we'll get lucky."

"God, I hope so." Her thoughts slipped back into suspicion like a dull toothache that refused to die.

Valdina is dirtier than you think.

A couple hours passed,,and the display of police presence finally dwindled down to Sheriff Stanton. With the house almost silent, Lauren heard the gentle hum of the ceiling fan from the living room. She glanced at her watch. Five-thirty. For the first time in years, the antique grandfather clock didn't chime.

Stanton walked to her, his movements stiff and awkward. "Damn wet weather. Really flares my arthritis. Well, looks like we're done in here. Two cops are posted outside. One out front. Another out back. No one's getting in or out without them knowing. "You'll be safe." He headed for the door. "We'll be working out front for a while yet. Make sure you lock up."

The second Stanton left, she flicked the deadbolt and slid the chain lock into place. Her gaze darted over the living room walls spattered and stained with red spray-paint. She wanted to be sick but to hell with the house. All she could think of was Eric and the look in his eyes while his partner lay bleeding to death.

Pete had looked as if he was dying and Lauren wasn't sure that he wasn't.

CHAPTER TWELVE

A t the hospital, Eric slammed the car in park and hopped out. They could tow the car. He didn't give a shit. Nurses dressed in white gathered on either side of the emergency doors. A small group of people huddled around a battered steel ashtray.

His muscles tensed. Sure, every day was a risk in his line of work. But this should never have happened. Not to Pete. Never. Guilt only added to Eric's frustration.

After flashing his badge at the desk nurse, he stared through the ER window. Pete appeared lifeless. He was half-naked on a gurney while a technician took x-rays. Members of the trauma unit gave him oxygen while others worked on him frantically.

It seemed like forever before a doctor met Eric in the hallway.

"How is he?"

"He's in critical condition. Has his family been notified?"

"I called his wife, Judy. She'll be here any minute."

"Okay. We're getting him prepped for surgery. He's lost a lot of blood and he's suffered a spinal cord injury from one of the bullets. It's not looking good."

Eric's heart sank.

The doctor continued. "My only concern at this point is getting the bleeding under control and keeping him alive."

"And his future?"

"If he makes it, he'll be a paraplegic and unfortunately that's not going to change." The doctor's eyes shifted to the ER. "I'm sorry but I have to go. They're ready for me. I'll speak with his wife after surgery."

"Doc?"

"Yes."

"Save him."

"I'll do what I can." The doctor repositioned his stethoscope around his neck and rushed down the hall.

Eric clenched one hand so tightly, he heard his fingers crack under the pressure.

This was his fault.

A thirty-four-year-old married man, his friend, his partner was paralysed. Christ, he wanted to bash the hell out of the ER door, and it took all his self-control not to.

Then he turned and saw Judy, her face white with panic against her long brown hair.

"Eric, where's Pete? Where's my husband?" She rushed past him and peered through the ER window. "Where is he?" Tears welled in her eyes and found their way down her cheeks.

He put his hand on her shoulder. "They just took him up to surgery."

He heard her quick gasp, her eyes searching his for answers.

"I don't understand. What happened?"

"He was shot." He paused for a moment. "It's bad, Judy."

Taking a deep unsteady breath, she stepped back from him. "No. How could this have happened?"

Because I sent Pete to Lauren's house. "I don't know but

Pete will pull through, Judy. He's young and strong. The doctors are doing everything they can. Come on, let's wait upstairs." He grasped her hand and they headed for the elevator.

On the second floor, Judy's knees buckled, and she collapsed into a chair. Eric paced from one end of the waiting room to the other. Minutes turned to hours. Bromstrom arrived with a half a dozen grim faced officers in his wake.

"How's Hallman. Is he going to make it?" Bromstrom asked.

Eric's mouth went dry like he hadn't swallowed in days. "He's paralysed from the waist down."

Bromstrom eyes widened. "Christ." He shook his head. "Does Judy know?"

"No, not yet."

"I spoke with Sheriff Stanton. Pete never had a chance. Did he say anything?" Bromstrom asked.

"He mentioned the van."

"I'm putting three more officers on this. We have to find that van. Stanton also said Lauren Taylor's house was broken into. I assume the two incidents are connected."

"More than likely. It's not surprising considering she received a death threat earlier today."

"Brennan, I want this lunatic caught before someone gets killed. Let me know if anything changes with Pete."

"I will." Eric heard a ding and the elevator doors opened. He turned to see Lauren.

Bromstrom walked away and joined the other officers in the waiting area.

"How's Pete?" she asked.

"He's in surgery." He kissed her forehead.

"What was that for?"

"Just glad you're here. Sorry to hear about your house."

"It's a mess, but it's just a house. I think that's the least of our worries right now."

He put his arm around her. "Listen, Pete's wife is here and some of the guys from the precinct. I'm sure Judy could use another woman to talk to. Do you mind?"

"Of course not. Whatever I can do to help."

Eric studied her as she introduced herself to Judy. Judy held Lauren's hand and cried while Lauren tried to comfort her. The sight ripped at Eric's heart and almost brought tears to his eyes.

This was his fault.

Hours passed before the doctor emerged to talk to Judy.

"Mrs. Hallman, I'm Doctor Mitchell."

Judy raised her head. "My husband. Is he okay?"

"He's in critical but stable condition. We were able to control the internal bleeding."

"Thank God." Judy breathed a loud sigh of relief.

"Three bullets were removed. Unfortunately, one bullet shattered his spine."

Judy gasped. "What?"

"Your husband has sustained a very serious spinal cord injury—he's lost the use of his legs. He's paralysed from the waist down."

"No!" Tears streamed down Judy's cheeks. "You're a doctor. You can fix him."

"I'm sorry, I know this is very difficult. Unfortunately, there is nothing more we can do. He has a long road ahead of him. Your husband can still have a very fulfilling life."

Judy stepped back and shook her head. "No. This can't be happening."

Lauren put her arm around Judy's shoulder.

"He'll be in recovery for a couple of hours, and then you can see him. He's not out of the woods yet. There is always the fear of infection after surgery. If you have any questions, please have the nurse page me. Again, I'm sorry."

Judy cried.

No one said a word. So silent in fact, Eric could hear the second hand of the huge wall clock click as each second passed.

Tears bordered Lauren's eyes. She clutched Judy's hand and glanced up at him.

Eric was amazed by the kindness Lauren had shown to a woman she'd never met before.

The tension in the room stretched even tighter over the next two and a half hours until a nurse finally summoned Judy to the recovery room.

Eric watched through the glass with Lauren standing next to him.

Judy ran to Pete's bedside and grabbed his hand. Monitors beeped and flashed. Another nurse took Pete's vital signs and checked the monitors.

"You already knew Pete was paralysed, didn't you?" Lauren asked.

He continued to watch Judy. "Yeah, how could you tell?"

"You were the only one in the room who wasn't shocked by the news."

"Guess I lost my poker face somewhere along the line. I didn't have the heart to tell Judy earlier."

"Pete's lucky to have you."

"Yeah, real lucky. If I hadn't sent him to your house, he wouldn't be lying in there." He knew his voice sounded angry.

Lauren clutched his hand. "This isn't your fault, Eric. You were doing your job. If it wasn't Pete, it would have been another officer, or even you. The only one to blame is the crazy person who pulled the trigger and that person is still out there."

His stomach flooded with nausea and anger. "Let's leave Judy alone for a bit. I need some air. How about you?"

"Me too."

Eric stepped outside the hospital and lit a cigarette. The rain had stopped, and a full moon lit the night sky. Lauren sat on the wooden bench while he paced back and forth.

"The stars seem brighter tonight." She pointed to the southeast. "Look at that one over there. It twinkles like a diamond."

He sat beside her and raised his head. "That's Jupiter, the fifth planet from the sun. When I was nine, my father used to tell me that Jupiter was the King of the Gods—ruler of Olympus. We'd spend hours together studying the stars and planets with the telescope he bought for my birthday. He was a real family man."

"I know you miss him. Duffy was one of the good guys. I wanted to call you after he died. I just didn't know what to say."

He put his arm around her shoulder. "I wish you had."

"I've never told anyone this, but I was at your father's funeral."

His eyes widened. "You were? I didn't see you."

"I stayed back from the crowd of officers and family. The moment I saw you, I cried. I couldn't bare your pain." She stood and swung her purse over her shoulder. "God,

I didn't realize it was getting so late. I really should get home. The trial's tomorrow."

"Do you need a ride? I can have one of the guys take you."

Lauren smiled. "Thanks, that's okay. I'll call a cab. If Judy needs anything, anything at all, let me know."

He reached out and caught her hand in his. For a long moment, he stared deep into her eyes. Without a word, he pulled her into his arms, her soft curves molding to his body. He kissed her, lingering, savouring the moment.

"You know Lauren, I was wrong. You really are a princess—and I mean that in a nice way."

* * *

Light filtered through the bedroom blinds. Eric listened to the traffic outside his apartment. Horns honked, tires screeched. He could hear yelling from across the street in Central Park. At three-thirty in the morning, the world appeared to be wide awake, just like him.

He hadn't had a drop of alcohol in four years, until tonight, not even after his father died. He rolled over in the bed. A half empty bottle of rum stared back at him, teasing, begging him to finish the bottle. What kind of life would Pete have bound to a wheelchair? And what about Judy? They were planning on having kids in the near future. Eric's guts churned, the feeling of guilt, overwhelming.

His hand trembled as he reached for the glass and gulped down the last swallow of rum. He stared at the empty glass and swung his legs over the side of the bed.

His mind froze. His body was numb. *What the hell am I doing?*

He could blow everything. Just when things were

looking up with his job...with Lauren. He grabbed the liquor bottle and headed for the kitchen, the floor cold against his bare feet. After riffling through the fridge, he located the last can of cola. Eric poured the remnants of the rum down the drain and took a gulp of pop.

He had to be there for Pete and he needed to protect Lauren.

CHAPTER THIRTEEN

Lauren lay in the warmth of the canopy bed and stared at the alarm clock. Bright scarlet digits gleamed back at her. Six fifteen. Her body ached. Her muscles throbbed with stiffness. After hours of cleaning last night, she had weeks of work ahead in the living room let alone the rest of the house.

The trial.

She jolted upright, and her head spun. Dazed, she glanced at the paperback that fell to the floor with a thud. She picked up the book and positioned it on the night stand beside the empty wine glass. Her head felt heavy as if she had drunk a bottle of wine instead of two glasses. With sluggish movements, her feet finally met the floor. She sat on the edge of the bed until she gathered enough strength to throw on her bathrobe.

Stillness engulfed the house. Too quiet.

"Lucy, where are you?"

Lauren waited.

The dog never came.

The rubber soles of her black slippers squeaked across the hardwood floor. In the foyer, Lucy sat at the front door whimpering.

"What's up girl? Come on, I'll let you out." The dog wagged her tail with such fury, Lauren's head started to spin.

Sunlight burst through the wispy clouds and shone down from the skylight in the kitchen. She narrowed her eyes and opened the patio doors. Lucy tore outside, her toenails scrapped against the ceramic floor like fingernails across a chalk board. The sound sent a shudder through Lauren's body.

"Cute dog," a male voice said.

Lauren's hand flew to her chest. "God. I forgot you were here."

She looked at the police officer. With a round baby face and huge green eyes, he looked like a teenager fresh out of school. Light hair shadowed his bottom lip. He didn't even look old enough to shave.

"Didn't mean to startle you."

"That's okay. How about some coffee, officer?"

His eyes lit at her words. "Call me, Tom. Sure. I could sure use some."

"Five minutes and it will be ready." She tightened the belt on her black silk robe and went back inside.

She put on a pot of coffee and yelled, "You up, Dad?"

No answer.

She went to the spare room and inched open the door. The curtains were drawn, the bed untouched. It wasn't the first time her father had pulled an over-nighter. Lauren remembered how he pretty much ate, drank and slept at the office last summer preparing for another high-profile murder trial. How a six-foot-two man slept on the hard leather sofa was beyond her. But he did. Pure dedication.

In the bathroom, she stroked rose colored blush

across her cheek bones then brushed her hair back into a ponytail and clasped it with a sterling emerald clip. Her eyes darted to her watch. She grabbed a white blouse and a tailored wool jacket with navy matching pants from her closet and got dressed. She sat in the wicker rocking chair and slipped on a pair of low heels.

When she stood up, a gold metal button popped off the jacket, bounced across the floor and rolled under the bed. "Shit. Not today." She looked at the jacket, and then at her closet. With little time to spare, she ripped the two remaining buttons off her jacket and tossed them in the pocket.

After letting Lucy in, she swung her purse over her shoulder, grabbed her brief case from under the bench in the foyer and opened the front door.

"Morning," the officer said, with a nod.

"Good Morning." She picked up the *New York Times* from the veranda, tucked the paper under her arm, and rushed down the stairs. "Oh, I left the doors unlocked. There's coffee on in the kitchen for you and Tom. I have to go into the city. It's trial day."

The officer flashed her a big smile. "Great. Thanks for the coffee and good luck. Hope Valdina goes down today."

Her sentiments exactly.

In the car, she quickly scanned the headlines of the paper. No surprise the news of the day took up the full front page.

Guilty of Murder? Or A Prosecutors Witch Hunt

Below, a picture of Gino Valdina and his lawyer, and another photograph of Troy, Lauren, and her father. The subtitle read:

Meet the Top Players

Lauren shook her head. Only the media could make a murder trial sound like a high stakes poker game.

Her heart skipped a beat and her fingers trembled as she guided the key into the ignition of the Mercedes. The last time she'd driven was the night of the accident. "You can do this. You have too."

With a long exhale she started the car and headed for Manhattan.

✽ ✽ ✽

Mid-morning sunbeams peaked atop the concrete and glass criminal court building. Lauren parked the car on Centre Street in the shadow of the tall structure and glanced at her watch one last time. Ten forty-five. The trial was set for eleven-fifteen.

She flipped through the newspaper to the horoscope section, a ritual since law school.

"You'll be in a caring mood today and will come to some serious conclusions about your relationship."

What relationship? She knew her feelings for Eric were still there and the prospect scared her to death. For years she'd gone out of her way to avoid a serious relationship, instead concentrated on her career. For the second time in her life, the detective with the riveting brown eyes and devilish grin knotted her emotions so tight, she wasn't sure if she could break free. She continued to read. "Be brave and do what your inner voice tells you to do. However, the planets warn you. Keep your guard up." Lauren shoved the paper to the passenger seat and exited the car.

On the courthouse steps, television, newspaper and

freelance journalists gathered.

A female reporter from CNN ran up to her and shoved a microphone in her face. "Miss Taylor. Any comments before the trial?"

"No comment." Lauren pushed the microphone away and continued up the steps. The same reporter tried again, but Lauren dodged her and finally made her way into the courthouse.

Inside security was tight. Two dozen officers huddled in groups of three and four, their gazes shifted from person to person.

The male officer smiled. "Morning."

"Good morning." She handed him her briefcase and purse. He flipped open the case and emptied her purse into a plastic container, searching the contents more diligently than usual, checking and rechecking each item.

When he was done, he picked up the metal detector. She held her arms up while he moved the wand up and down one side of her body, and then the other. The detector went off. Loud beeps echoed throughout the lobby.

Heads turned.

An officer stepped in front of her. For a moment she stiffened. Damn, the buttons.

"Empty your pockets," he ordered.

She felt her face flush. Lauren pulled the gold-coloured buttons from her pocket and handed them to him. "Sorry. I forgot."

She watched the officer inspect them. "They're from my jacket."

He stepped aside and handed the buttons back to her. "Okay, go ahead."

"Thank you." She shot him a small smile, but he never moved a muscle, instead continued to stare ahead like a statue.

The narrow hallway of the courthouse was cluttered with navy and black suits. A small tour group of high-school aged students rushed by. Lauren shook her head surprised they'd allow a tour when the building would be filled with members of New York's most deadly crime syndicate ready to support Gino Valdina in any way.

Two large uniformed court officers stood guard outside of the room.

Dressed in an expensive black suit and two-toned red and yellow striped tie, Troy leaned against the wall with his jaw clenched.

He rushed to her, his eyes cold looking and hard. "It's about time you got here."

Now a victim of his glare, the sarcasm of his remark irritated her. "Calm down, Troy. We have lots of time."

His jaw clenched tighter. "Where the hell is your father?" His voice lowered to a harsh whisper. "The trial of the century and he's not here."

"What do you mean he's not here? I thought he stayed at the office last night and came in with you."

He let out a long audible breath. "I have no idea what you're talking about. I haven't been to the office since I got back from the Bahamas. I had our files sent over."

Panic invaded her body. Dad was never late. Ever. Maybe he's stuck in traffic? She felt Troy's hand on her arm. He half escorted her, half pushed her into the now open courtroom. *Arrogant jerk.*

She took a seat at the prosecution's table. Troy pulled up a chair beside her.

He rested his arms against the dark wood table. "He'd

better get here soon."

"He'll be here." She glanced over her shoulder.

Within minutes the courtroom gallery filled with spectators, media members, the curious and some familiar members of the Valdina crime family.

Dad, where are you?

In the row behind Lauren, Madelina's mother and the rest of her family sat. Lauren felt a deep sense of sorrow at their loss. A feeling she knew all too well.

Lauren looked at the tall man dressed in a dark brown Armani suit escorted by two court officers to the defense table. People whispered. Some gasped. Gino Valdina took a seat and leaned back in the chair. His lawyer stood next to him along with the rest of his defense team.

Each time the courtroom door squeaked open, the sound echoed through the wood paneled walls. Heads turned, including hers.

"Please rise," the bailiff said.

A male clerk jumped to his feet and straightened his tie. The room fell silent. Everyone stood.

The judge entered as his black robe flapped behind him. He took a seat and gave the bailiff a quick nod.

"The court is now in session. The Honorable Judge Walter Brookstein presiding. Please be seated," the bailiff said.

Lauren glanced over her shoulder at the closed door. *God, where is he? Dad would never miss this trial...*

"In the matter of the State of New York versus Gino Valdina," the court clerk cried out, "the charge being one count of murder in the first degree. A plea of not guilty has been entered."

The judge glanced up through his heavy thick-rimmed glasses and stared at Lauren. "Are we ready?"

She stood and addressed the court. "Yes, Your Honor."

Judge Brookstein's lips thinned while his gaze shifted to the defense table.

Ricardo Pinstronna rose. "Ready for the defense, Your Honor."

"Bailiff, please bring in the jury."

From the side door, the jury of seven women and five men paraded to the jury box and took their seats.

The judge leaned back in his chair. "Miss Taylor, you have the floor."

Lauren stood and smoothed her jacket. "The State will prove beyond a reasonable doubt that Gino Valdina committed the vicious murder of his wife, Madelina Valdina." She strolled in front of the jury box and stopped. "You're going to hear the term, "reasonable doubt" various times throughout this trial. This means the state's version of the crime is supported by testimony and evidence which will convince you Gino Valdina, in fact, killed his wife. The evidence will leave you with no reasonable doubt that the crime was committed by Mr. Valdina. The State will show that Gino Valdina, not only killed his wife, he killed her in cold blood and with premeditation."

For the next ten minutes, Lauren put on the show of her life. A show it was. Animated and exaggerated movements she learned from watching her father's trials until she completed her opening statement.

Ricardo Pinstronna stood.

Madelina's mother pounced to her feet and pointed at Gino Valdina. "Murderer! You killed my daughter. Dirty rotten murderer!"

The judge slammed down his gavel. "Order in this court. Remove that woman now."

One of the burly court officers grabbed the woman's arm and partially dragged and partially ushered her to the double doors.

Tears rolled down the woman's cheeks. "He's a murderer. He killed my daughter." She raised her arm and pointed at Valdina. "I hope you rot in hell."

Judge Brookstein pounded down his gavel again. "I won't have my court room turned into a circus. Clear the room. Thirty-minute recess."

Lauren sighed.

Gino Valdina's black eyes met hers. He winked. The look on his face sent a shiver through her body. She caught the handle of her briefcase and hurried to the door. In the hallway, she opened her briefcase, pulled out her cell phone and dialed the office.

One ring. Two.

"For God sakes, pick up the phone Marie."

Three. Four. Five rings.

"You've reached the Manhattan District Attorney's Office. If you know your party's number, please dial it now. For a departmental listing press one. If you are a victim of a crime press two. If this is an emergency, please hang up and call 9-1-1.

You've got to be kidding me. Lauren hung up and tried again.

"Good Morning. Manhattan District Attorney's Office."

"Marie, it's Lauren. Is my father there?"

"Oh, Lauren. Nice to hear from you. How's the trial going?"

Lauren tapped her foot on the floor and was about to lose her patience. "It's going fine. I really need to talk to my father. Now Marie."

"I haven't seen him. Isn't he with you?"

Lauren's heart pounded. "I thought he slept there last night."

"Not that I know of. He hasn't been in since—"

"When Marie?" Lauren cradled the phone under her chin.

"He dropped in for about an hour on Tuesday."

"Tuesday? Are you sure, Marie? This is Thursday. He left for the office yesterday afternoon.

"I'm absolutely sure. Stephen never showed up here."

❋ ❋ ❋

When Lauren arrived at the office, the trial division of the Manhattan District Attorney's office was relatively quiet considering there were over thirty district attorneys and legal and supervisory staff working on dozens of cases at a time from misdemeanors to felony crimes.

No chance in hell would her father miss this trial. More than anything, he wanted to see Gino where he belonged. Behind bars for life. She had the same deep hollow emptiness in her heart she felt the night her brother died. *Something is wrong. Very wrong.*

"Get Max Richards on the phone."

"The private investigator?" Marie asked.

"Yes." Lauren retrieved her messages from the desk and scanned through them before slipping them into her jacket pocket.

Marie lowered her gaze and peeked up through a mop of long black curls. "I know I haven't been here long, but I have a good sense when something's not right."

You and me both.

"Thanks. I appreciate your concern, Marie. I really can't talk right now. I'll be in Dad's office."

If anyone could find her father, Lauren prayed Max could—the only investigator her father trusted. She halted in the doorway of the massive office. Her father's L-shape cherry desk sat untouched. She parked herself in the vintage high-back chair and ran her hand over the leather inserts of the desk. *Please be safe, Dad.*

Marie popped her head inside the door. "Max is on line four."

Lauren drew a deep breath and picked up the phone. "Max, my father didn't show up for the trial. I've called the house and the cabin a dozen times in the past hour. He left me a note yesterday saying he was coming to the office. I just assumed he slept here. He never showed up, Max. I'm worried sick."

"Okay, try to stay calm. I'll check around and see what I can find out. I'll get back to you."

The concern she heard in his voice, the way his voice was pinched, made her worry even more.

"Max?"

"Yeah."

"We will find him, won't we?"

"Yes."

The phone on the other end went silent.

Lauren swallowed the lump in her throat and turned the chair to face the window.

The city looked even larger from the twenty-second floor. Concrete and glass ruled the skyline. Empty numbness surged in the pit of her stomach. *He's out there somewhere.*

"Any news?"

She dug her fingernails into the padded arm of the chair and spun the chair around. "Troy, what are you doing here. What about the trial?"

He set his briefcase on the floor and tossed his jacket over the arm of the couch. "Richardo was bitching about not having the witness list in time so Brookstein adjourned until tomorrow morning."

Lauren wasn't convinced that leaving Troy in the 'lead chair' was the best thing to do but she didn't have a choice. He knew the case and had the most experience. God, he'd be on an ego trip for months.

"That's just ridiculous. He's had more than enough time." She stood and glanced at the mahogany bookcase crammed with old law books her father had collected over the years. "I still haven't heard from Dad. I just got off the phone with Max Richards."

The second she mentioned Max's name Troy snatched up his jacket and briefcase.

"If you hear anything, call me."

She'd never seen him move so fast. Just plain weird. "Something I said?"

"I have to get going." He avoided making eye contact and grasped her arm, his fingers lingering too long. "Let me know if you hear anything."

❊ ❊ ❊

Eric slowed the Mustang to a crawl and searched the street for his informant, Jimmy Flame. This part of Brooklyn had it all—graffiti and gangs—a snake pit of hell where debts were paid in blood. Lots of blood. As it turned out, he spotted the lanky twenty-something-drug-dealer strolling up the sidewalk.

Eric didn't trust the scar-faced kid dressed in clothes three sizes too big, but Jimmy knew the streets and somehow had stayed clear of the gangs. A real miracle. He also knew Jimmy would be discreet if he knew what was good for him.

Eric pulled the car over and stopped. Jimmy looked him square in the eye, turned, and kept walking.

Eric jumped out of the car and snatched the back of Jimmy's shirt. "We need to talk." He whirled him around.

"Hey, you promised you'd only come around at night." Jimmy scanned up and down the street clearly worried someone might see him with a cop.

"It's important. Get in."

Jimmy hopped into the car and scrunched down low in the passenger seat.

Eric started the engine and glanced at Jimmy's low riding jeans. "How the hell can you wear those baggy ass pants? They should be outlawed."

"What man? You don't like my gear? These pants are cool." Jimmy ran his hand over his knee. "What's so important?"

"Heard anything about prosecutor Stephen Taylor or the new district attorney?" Jimmy kept one hand clutched on the door handle.

Convinced the kid might bolt if he had the chance, Eric sped up.

"I ain't heard nothing on the DA, but—"

"If you know something, spit it out. I'm not in the mood for games." Eric looked at him. Jimmy's shaved head glistened with sweat in the early morning sun.

"Man, you're gonna get me killed." Jimmy sank back into the seat, his fingers tightened around the handle of the door. "Some dude was looking for someone to put the scare into Taylor and the DA. I never saw him, but one of my boys told the guy to hit the road. The deal didn't smell right. Something was way off."

"How did Paul Cassico end up dead?"

Jimmy lit a cigarette and took an extra-long drag. "Cassico is a small-time bookie, you know, neighborhood shit, horse races, and fights. Valdina learned the guy would be cooperating with the feds so Valdina had one of his crew take him out."

"Did Cassico ever mention who killed my father?"

"The stupid shit went around flappin' his gums. Said he knew who shot the cop in the warehouse drug deal. He also said he'd make a large stash when he went to the cops."

Eric's heart pounded. "Did he give a name, Jimmy?"

"Nope."

"Shit. I need to find the shooter."

"I don't wanna get involved with Valdina's crew. You're talking Mafia." Jimmy shook his head.

"Man. I'm too young to die."

Eric could tell by the quiver in the kid's voice, he was scared. Something he'd never seen before. "Has someone threatened you?"

"Not yet. They will as soon as I start asking questions."

"You're smart. You'll find a way to get the info. Besides, if you piss me off, I'll drag your drug-pedalling ass off to jail. You understand?"

Jimmy remained silent for a moment. "Man, you're a hard-ass."

"Find out what you can." Eric steered the car into an empty parking lot and tossed fifty bucks at him. "I'll be back in a couple of days and watch your back."

As Eric pulled away, he heard Jimmy call him an asshole. Okay, he deserved that. And yeah, he was tough on the kid when he needed to be. It was all part of the job. He liked Jimmy, but he'd never admit it. From what he just witnessed, Jimmy was scared and that worried Eric even more.

CHAPTER FOURTEEN

Midtown South Precinct choked with commotion like evening rush hour in Manhattan. Keyboards clicked, phones rang, voices chattered. Fluorescent lights buzzed and flickered overhead.

"I'm here to see Detective Brennan," Lauren shouted above the racket.

The desk sergeant glanced at the wall clock beside him. "Sorry, Brennan's not here. Something I can help you with?"

"I need to file a missing person's report."

"Just a second." The sergeant turned and yelled to the stocky man with a bald, shiny head. "Hey, Greyson."

The man nodded and came to greet her.

With a toothpick hanging from his mouth, he held his hand out to her. "Nick Greyson. Oh, sorry. I just quit smoking."

"Lauren Taylor." She shook his hand.

"I know who you are. Come with me."

She followed him into Interview Room One.

"Have a seat." He closed the door and then sat across from her.

For the next twenty minutes, she told her story.

When she was done, Greyson stood and stretched his legs. "I'll need you to a sign permission form, first. You do understand we wait forty-eight hours before starting a search?"

Bile crept up her throat and she swallowed it. "Yes. But after everything that's happened, couldn't you make an exception? Detective Brennan knows what is going on. Please talk with him."

"Brennan's homicide. I'm in charge of missing persons."

Not a good sign. Just what she needed. A guy with a big-time attitude.

He leaned back in the chair. "Look. We have procedures to follow. Adults *are* allowed to go missing, Miss Taylor. Believe me, hundreds do every day."

"Haven't you heard anything I just said? He's the Deputy District Attorney for God sakes. He'd never miss the Valdina trial."

Greyson popped the toothpick out of his mouth and placed it on the desk. "Is there any reason your father might want to disappear? Problems at work? His personal life?"

"Are you crazy?" She slammed her fist on the table. "You have a lot of nerve to ask."

"I'm not trying to be difficult here. From where I sit, it's not the first time a person has wanted to vanish."

"Not my father." She scooped her purse from the table and swung it over her shoulder. "You're wrong. Give me that damn permission form."

He passed the form across the table which she snatched from his hand and scribbled her signature on the bottom.

"Miss Taylor, please..."

Lauren flung open the door and stomped out of the room.

Outside the sun had set and time was running out. She needed help.

* * *

Two hours, a lukewarm coffee and a half a pack of cigarettes later, Eric arrived at the hospital to check on Pete. At eleven in the morning, the parking lot was full. He flashed his badge at the security guard who gave him a half-cocked grin then motioned him to park in the reserved employee section.

The main lobby clamoured with activity and drowned out the loud grumble of his stomach, a clear sign his morning caffeine wasn't sitting too well. After a visit to the gift shop and a fistful of antacid tablets, his gut finally settled. Armed with a bag of Pete's favorites— Twinkies, potato chips, chocolate bars, and a variety of fishing magazines—Eric inhaled a deep breath and took the elevator to the fourth floor.

From the doorway, Eric spied Judy standing by the window dressed in a tan ribbed sweater and short plaid skirt. She looked like a pixie; fine boned, petite, and appeared defeated.

He fought to put on a happy face. Christ, how could he pretend to be happy? He'd ruined his partner's life.

When all was said and done, Eric wondered if his best friend would blame him as much as he blamed himself.

Judy turned and looked at him, her face pale and tense. "I'm glad you're here."

He walked into the room. "How's he doing?"

"A tad better. Dr. Mitchell said he's coming along well

considering. He's still pretty groggy, but they removed the breathing tube early this morning. That's a good sign —isn't it?"

"Yeah, it is." He set the bag of goodies on the chair next to the bed.

It looked like everyone Pete knew had sent flowers. Carnations, tiger lilies, a powder blue basket full of happy ass daisies. God, how Eric hated flowers. A waste of money and a sad reminder that everything dies.

"How are you holding up?"

Judy gave a tired sigh. "I'm okay. Pete's mother and brother are flying in from Las Vegas tomorrow afternoon. So, I've got to keep the old chin up. I'll have a houseful."

She stepped away from the window and whispered in his ear. "Pete doesn't know he's paralysed. They have him pretty drugged up. The doctor felt it would be best to tell him once his overall condition improves."

"I won't say anything." Eric glanced over her shoulder to see two green eyes staring at him. "He's awake."

Pete reached for him.

"Hey, there partner." Eric leaned over the bed. "You gave me one hell of a scare. Am I glad to see you."

"Shot me."

"I know."

Pete licked his lips. "Van."

"I'll find who did this. I promise." Eric grabbed the paper bag of goodies. "Hey look what I brought you. Twinkies, chocolate, all the stuff Judy doesn't like you to eat."

His partner smiled. "Thanks, man."

He watched Pete try to hold the bag. His arm trembled from weakness and the bag slid to the bed.

Eric curled his hand into a rigid fist, anger threatened

to choke him. This was his fault. He had to find the driver of the van.

Judy kissed Pete's hand. "You'd better rest. The doctor wants you to take it easy. I'll be right back."

Pete's eyelids grew heavy and closed before Judy finished talking.

In the hallway, she leaned against the wall. "Please thank Lauren for me. I don't know what I'd have done last night without her kindness."

"I will."

"I know it's none of my business but—"

"You're going to do your matchmaking thing again." He couldn't help but smile.

Her eyes lit. "You two were made for each other. Trust me."

"Jude, I appreciate your faith but there's a lot of baggage attached to both of us. Got a lot of unpacking to do before we can move forward."

"You'll figure it out." She gave him a peck on his check. "I'd better get back. Remember what I said about Lauren. And Eric…I'm never wrong."

As he left the room, a young woman approached him carrying an enormous arrangement of flowers.

She peeked through the bouquet. "Is this Mr. Hallman's room?"

Christ, not more. Ugly ones at that. "Yeah, I'll take them." Eric watched the woman disappear past the nurse's station before he headed back into the room.

Judy's eyes widened. "I thought you left?"

"These just arrived."

Judy looked at the bouquet and her lips twisted. "They look like something Pete's mother would send. Only Marge would mix carnations and a black rose together. The woman has no taste. Do me a favour, Eric. Can you open the card? I really don't want to deal with anymore flowers or cards right now."

He flipped open the flap of the small white envelope and slid out a yellow card with handwriting on it.

These flowers will die and so will you.

Judy looked at him briefly, her eyes red and swollen from hours of crying. "Was I right? Are they from, Marge?"

Not unless your mother-in-law's the world's worst poet. "No, wrong room, Judy. I'll take them next door for you."

* * *

Eric rushed down the hallway and stuck his head around the corner and peered both ways. The woman who'd delivered the flowers was long gone.

He stopped and talked to the security guard posted outside Pete's room. "Nothing goes in this room without being thoroughly searched. Keep your eyes open for anything or anyone that seems out of place." Eric paused for a moment before continuing. "No visitors, except for Officer Hallman's wife and immediately family members. Make sure you get ID and log each visitor."

"You got it," the guard said.

Eric glanced at the bouquet and card clutched in his hand. Anger ripped through his veins. "I'll have a couple NYPD officers relieve you within the hour."

As Eric left the hospital, the words on the card echoed through his mind.

These flowers will die and so will you.

He'd swing by the lab and hopefully, the guys could get a fingerprint or discover where the flowers were purchased. Whoever did this to Pete wasn't through yet. Eric needed to find that van.

❋ ❋ ❋

Manhattan's upper west side pulsated with traffic. Blocks away on Central Park West, Lauren parked the Mercedes and got out. The cool north breeze made her shiver. She pulled her sweater closed and quickened her pace. Across the street, teenagers crowded together like starving animals around a street vendor's cart. The mouth-watering aroma of hotdogs made her stomach growl.

In front of the 19th century Brownstone, an iron lamppost cast a soft yellow light against the rustic brick.

On the second-floor landing, soft rock music flowed through the hall, the melody familiar. She rapped on the door. *Please be home.*

The door opened. Eric stood shirtless with a white towel draped around his shoulders, dressed in blue jeans. Water dripped from his brown hair and trickled down his neck.

His eyes widened, and he smiled. "Lauren."

"Dad never showed up for the trial."

His smile disappeared. "What?" He grabbed her hand. "Come in."

In the living room, her knees crumpled, and she collapsed on the couch. "Eric, I'm scared to death."

"God, you're shaking."

Deep lines worked across Eric's forehead. He was as worried as she was. For the next twenty minutes, Lauren went through the events that led to her father's disappearance.

"Okay. Is there any way we can get a look at your father's files?"

"You don't think Valdina is involved?"

"I'm not saying he's not. I'd like to look at the files and see if we can figure out what the hell is going on. You ready to get to work?"

"Yes." She took a long deep breath and her voice strengthened. "We'll have to go to the office because all my files at home were destroyed."

"Okay, let me grab a shirt." His eyes met hers. "Be right back."

For the first time all day she felt a strange numbed comfort. She stood and stretched her legs.

An overhead crystal chandelier hung from the high ceiling and made the hardwood floors shine like glass. Deep mustard painted walls highlighted the white mantel around the gas fireplace. She stared at a photograph on the mantel, a picture of her and Eric at her father's cabin. *We looked so happy. Too bad it ended.*

"Ready?" Eric asked.

"I'm surprised you've kept this picture of us."

"It's my favorite photo. Amanda should have been a photographer."

Lauren slid her fingers along the edge of the frame. "Yeah, we'd better get moving."

❊ ❊ ❊

In the heart of Manhattan, neon lights twinkled atop the Ethel Barrymore Theatre. Musical lovers filled the sidewalks of the theatre district ready to enter the nine o'clock show.

Eric glanced at Lauren. "You want to go see a Broadway show sometime?"

At first, she wasn't sure if he was serious or not but decided to play along. "A movie maybe, not Broadway."

"I thought women liked musicals. Your mother was an actress, wasn't she?" He turned off the radio and rolled down the window.

Lauren cringed. "It's just not something I enjoy, okay? Can we drop it?"

He lit a cigarette and took a long drag. "Sure." Her face showed signs of a strange tension the way her forehead crinkled. "Are you okay? You look pale." Then he heard her stomach growl. "Sounds like you're starving."

"I can't eat. All I want is to find my father. Eric, what if he's dead?"

He reached over and held her hand. "You can't think like that. We'll find him."

Across the street, a man with long greasy hair stood beside a garbage can.

Eric slowed the car and took another look. His heart went wild and pounded against his chest. Adrenalin kicked in and for a moment he swore he stopped breathing. The man turned, looked directly at him, and then bolted in the other direction.

The birthmark on the man's face. "You're not getting away this time you bastard." Eric clobbered the brakes. The Mustang squealed to a stop.

Lauren clawed the dashboard with both hands. "What's—?"

"That's the piece of crap who killed my father." He raced into the opposite lane, whizzing in and out of traffic.

Headlights approached the car, fast.

"Watch out, Eric!"

He gripped the steering wheel and swerved out of the way. "Hang on, Lauren. Shit. Where did he go?"

She pointed to a darkened alley. "There."

Eric made a right sharp turn. Tires screamed. The smell of scorched rubber and gas filled the car. At the end of the alley, the guy tried to climb a chain link fence and plummeted to the ground. He scrambled to his feet and tried to scale the fence again.

Eric hurled the car into park and jumped out.

Anger pumped through his veins, muscles flinched through his shirt. He stopped, planted his feet firmly on the uneven ground, and aimed his .38 at the guy's back. "Get down asshole! Now!"

The man slid to the ground then froze like a statue.

"Just give me a reason to shoot." Eric's finger shook and touched the cold steel trigger ready to fire. "Put your hands up."

The man raised his arms above his head.

Eric took a step and kept his gun aimed. "If you even breathe the wrong way, I'll kill you." He slipped his gun into his pocket, grabbed the man's hands and twisted them behind him.

"Jesus, you're hurting me."

Eric secured the handcuffs around the man's wrists. "You think this hurts? Just wait." He slammed the guy's face into the chain-link fence. "What's your name?"

"Anthony." He gasped for a breath. "Benigno."

Eric flung him around. "Well Anthony, today is your lucky day."

"What?"

"This." Eric threw a right punch square on the guy's jaw. Bones crackled and popped.

Benigno wobbled and then hit the asphalt.

"That's for my father. This is from me." Eric kicked him hard in the ribs. So hard, the guy's ribs snapped and crunched.

The guy groaned and curled into a ball. "Stop. Please stop!"

"Then tell me who you work for."

Eric kicked him again. "Who?"

Anthony rolled onto his back and clutched his stomach. "Gino—Valdina."

Eric dove to his knees and wrapped his hands around the man's neck. "You killed my father and now I'm going to squeeze the life out of you."

"Don't kill me—please," Anthony whimpered.

Eric's fingernails penetrated the man's sweaty neck, clutching tighter and tighter.

Benigno's dark eyes widened and bulged. He gulped for a breath.

Footsteps pounded behind him.

Eric glanced over his shoulder. "Lauren, stay back. This doesn't concern you."

"Eric, don't do this. Think of your future."

"Get back in the car."

"You're going to kill him. Look at him. He's turning blue. You'll lose everything."

"He should have thought about that before he gunned down my father. The low-life piece of shit deserves to die."

Lauren dropped to the ground beside him. "I'm begging you, Eric, please. Duffy wouldn't want you to do this. You're a cop for God sakes. Let go of him. Do this the right way...I care about you."

Eric thought about the promise he made to his mother as Lauren's words played in his head. His grip slowly loosened around Anthony's neck. He let go.

Anthony sputtered, spit and moaned.

Eric rose and kicked an empty cardboard box across

the alley. Then he smiled, satisfied he had his father's killer.

Ten minutes later, Eric watched the squad car leave with Benigno inside.

He'd caught the bastard.

He turned to Lauren. "Thank you. You're were right. The piece of shit isn't worth my job or my life." With a long sigh of relief, he put his arm around her shoulder. "Come on. Let's find your father."

CHAPTER FIFTEEN

L auren never believed bad things happened in threes until now. The accident. Pete. Her father. She shuddered at the thought and dug deep into her file cabinet. Soft music played throughout the office's concealed speakers as a full moon glistened against the window and lit the city below.

"Okay, here they are. I probably shouldn't be showing you these but it's an emergency. I'll deal with the possible consequences later." She dropped a pile onto Eric's lap.

"Thanks. Here you take this half and I'll work through these."

She snatched the folders and sat on the floor in front of the couch beside him. "I don't know. I think this might be a waste of time."

"We need to start somewhere."

He scanned the contents of each folder. Dark circles shadowed his eyes. He'd always worked so hard, giving his all to his job. She'd never seen the side of him she'd seen tonight. So angry. So vengeful. A look she never wanted to see again.

He rolled up his sleeves. "Did you mean what you said earlier?"

The question sent her pulse spinning. "About what?" She kept her eyes lowered and pretended to read.

"That you cared about me. Or were you just trying to stop me from killing Benigno?"

"Both." She swallowed the lump in her throat and flipped to the next file folder. As much as she didn't want to admit it, she still cared for him deeper than she wanted to, and probably always would.

The phone rang.

She slid across the floor and grabbed the phone from her desk. "Hello? Max, God, I'm so glad you called. Hang on. I'm going to put you on the loud speaker." She pressed the speaker button. "Okay, go ahead."

"Word on the street is Gino hired someone to scare you and your father by running you off the road. He's pissed off and pretty desperate. I haven't heard anything about the shooting at the grocery store which leads me to believe the two incidents might not be connected."

Eric's eyebrows rose. "I hope you're wrong."

"Lauren, who's that?" Max asked.

"Eric Brennan, a detective with Midtown South. We're looking through some past cases trying to find a possible clue to my father's disappearance."

"Find anything?"

"Nothing yet."

"Keep looking. We'll find him."

"Thanks, Max"

"And Eric, take care of Lauren."

"Oh, I will," Eric said.

She hung up the phone and shoved the folders across the floor. "There's nothing in these. Damn it. How hard is it to find a full-grown man on crutches? He can't disappear into thin air."

Eric touched her hand. "Look, I know you're scared but we have to keep looking. Who is this Max guy?"

"A private detective. We use his services here at the office. My father and Max have been friends since their college days."

By two in the morning, her eyelids kept closing. She stood and stretched her legs hoping to shake off her exhaustion. It didn't work. They'd searched all her cases and partially through her father's most recent cases. Nothing so far.

"Why don't you rest for a while? I'll keep reading."

She yawned. "You sure you don't mind?"

Eric stroked the side of her face. "Go ahead."

She stretched out on the couch and closed her eyes. Sleep. She needed sleep.

The last thing Lauren heard was Eric say, "I care about you too."

❅ ❅ ❅

"Rise and shine sleeping beauty. Well isn't this a cozy little scene." Troy said.

Lauren kept her eyes shut. *Maybe the jerk will go away.* "Get lost. I've been up most of the night."

"And I thought you were all work and no play, Lauren."

She opened her eyes. "What the hell are you talking about?" Then she realized Eric was beside her sleeping and snoring softly. "It's not what it looks like. Besides I don't need to explain myself to you."

Troy puffed out his chest. "Call it what you want. Looks good to me."

"Get out of my office."

"Boy, you're bitchy in the morning."

She shot him a cold stare. "Any word about my father?"

"Nothing. I wouldn't worry too much, though. He'll

turn up."

"I hope you're right."

Troy smiled. "Don't you have more important things to worry about than cuddling up with him?"

Now he was irritating her even more. "Go away, Troy. Now, please."

She heard the office door slam closed. *Jerk.*

Eric stirred. His hand slid around her waist and he pulled her body close, molding her body into his. She lay in his arms conscious of the strength and warmth of his flesh, the smell of his skin, his warm breath against the back of her neck. She hadn't felt like this in years. Safe and protected.

He whispered against her ear. "Guess I fell asleep too. What time is it?"

"Six-fifteen."

He slid his body over hers, stopped and gazed into her eyes. "God, you're beautiful."

She thought he was going to kiss her when a loud rap at the door startled her. "Just a minute."

Eric rose then sat on the edge of her desk.

She jolted upright on the couch, smoothed her hair and straightened her sweatshirt. "Come in."

The door flew open.

"Amanda!" Lauren bounced off the couch and threw her arms around Amanda's neck and hugged her. "Boy, I'm so glad to see you."

"I called your house a dozen times last night. Then I dropped by. Cops were everywhere. What the heck is happening?" Her eyes widened. "Eric?"

"Hi"

"My goodness. We have some catching up to do, Lauren." Amanda smiled at her with an air of approval.

"Dad's missing."

Amanda's eyebrows rose. "Missing? No, I saw him yesterday morning."

"You saw him?" Lauren asked.

"Yeah, at about nine o'clock, out front. I think he got into a van."

Lauren gasped. "Oh, no."

Eric put his arm around her shoulder. "It's going to be okay."

"I don't understand. Is something wrong? Stephen said he knew the driver."

Lauren winced. "That can't be." Her gaze shifted to Eric.

Eric stood. "I think you'd better fill me in, Amanda."

Amanda sat on the couch, fidgeting with her hair. For the next five minutes, she kept her eyes glued to Eric. "God, I can't believe so much has happened while I was on vacation. We have to find Stephen." She stood and smoothed the flowered print mini skirt around her hips. "What can I do to help?"

"I need a list of people that Stephen deals with on a daily basis. Lawyers, clerks, judges."

"You got it," Amanda said.

"Lauren, can you get me the names of your father's friends and any women he's dated in the last few years?"

"Of course."

"Then I want you to go home and wait. Take Amanda with you," he said.

"What about you? What are you going to do?"

"I need to get to the hospital and check on Pete. Eric glanced at his watch. "How about we meet at your house, say around noon?"

"Okay." Lauren walked him to the door, her mind a

crazy mixture of hope and fear. "Please be careful."

* * *

While Amanda used the washroom, Lauren waited in the main lobby and ran into Max. He greeted her with a warm smile. At sixty-five, he didn't look a day over forty. His fair skin magnified his hazel eyes and dark brown hair.

"Glad I caught you." He gave her a hug. "How are you doing?"

"I'm worried sick, Max."

He followed her to a couch situated next to the elevators and sat.

Lauren remained standing.

He flipped open the lid of his briefcase. "Me too. Listen, this may have nothing to do with Stephen's disappearance but two weeks ago he asked me to look into a possible internal issue within the district attorney's office."

"Internal issue? What are you talking about?"

He handed her a cream coloured file folder. "You need to read this especially now with your father missing."

She took the folder and read the contents.

"You have got to be kidding. Troy took a seven-hundred-thousand-dollar payoff from Gino Valdina?" Her knees went weak. She grabbed the edge of the couch to steady herself. "I know Troy's an arrogant, self-centered jerk. But I can't believe this."

Gino Valdina is dirtier than you think.

"God, Max. Valdina's lawyer tried to warn me. I thought he was threatening me so I blew him off. That's what Richardo was trying to tell me. He knew all along."

Max looked her straight in the eye. "It gets worse.

Your father suspected Troy had been working in Valdina's camp for some time. The payoff was to make sure incriminating evidence disappeared from the police department's evidence room. Evidence which proved Valdina was home that night."

Troy? Evidence tampering? Lauren couldn't believe what she was hearing. Bile rose up her throat. She forced it back down. "What evidence?"

"The murder weapon. The knife used to kill Madelina."

"Oh, my God. I never had a chance in hell of winning this case. Troy made damn sure of that." Lauren sat on the couch. "Gino *has* to have something on Troy, right? Troy would never put his career in jeopardy like this. Ever. He's too much of an egotistical bastard."

She knew by the look on Max's face, she was right. There was more to the story.

"Lauren, he was sleeping with Gino's wife."

She threw her hands up in the air. "Now I've heard it all. What an idiot. This is unbelievable." Troy's sudden exit from the office when he learned Lauren had contacted Max all made sense. He was spooked knowing Max might uncover the truth.

Lauren shook her head. "So instead of killing Troy, Gino killed his wife and kept Troy alive knowing a district attorney would be more helpful alive than dead and Gino would get away with murder—again."

"Exactly. And if Troy didn't play along, he knew Gino would kill him next."

Lauren stood, clutching the file folder cursing herself for not seeing through Troy. "We have to go to the police. They aren't getting away with this. I'll make damn sure of it."

Max rubbed his forehead. "I'm not sure that's a good idea. What if Troy is involved in your father's disappearance?"

* * *

Outside the office tower, Eric stood in a patch of sunlight smoking a cigarette. He had to find Stephen and now. The first forty-eight hours were crucial, and time had run out.

A jade metallic Porsche pulled up and parked in front of the building. Right away he recognized the assistant district attorney. Eric shook his head and laughed under his breath. For a guy in his late forties, Troy looked like an aging rock star with bleached blonde hair. He swore the guy wore eyeliner.

Troy spotted him and grinned. "Have a nice little cuddle with Lauren, detective?"

"That's none of your business." Eric blew smoke in the man's face, and then tossed the butt on the sidewalk. "Any reason you would want Stephen to disappear?"

"What the hell kind of question is that? I don't have to listen to this crap." Troy stepped forward.

Eric blocked him. "I've never liked you. Just watch yourself. If your name comes up at all, you'll wish you'd never meet me."

The man's beady eyes darted back and forth, and his jaw twitched. "Go catch some bad guys or something. Don't you have better things to do than threaten me?"

Eric laughed. "I'm not threatening you." He patted Troy on the shoulder and stepped to one side. "Man, learn to relax."

Troy marched by him like a kid scolded by his mother.

Eric chuckled. What a loser.

✳ ✳ ✳

Eric parked his car at the back of the hospital and slipped through the restricted entrance. Hand-drawn pictures of clowns and stick figures crowded the cheerful sky, blue walls of the pediatric wing. Nurses dressed in bright coloured uniforms wandered in and out of rooms. Inside the elevator, he pressed the button to the second floor.

The corridor buzzed with staff. At the end of the hall, he nodded at the two uniformed officers before poking his head in Pete's room.

The bed was empty.

He quickly found a nurse. "Where's Pete Hallman?"

"Are you family?"

He pulled out his badge and flashed it to her. "No."

"Mr. Hallman is in emergency surgery."

Worry rapped up his spine. "What happened?"

The nurse shrugged. "I don't know. I just started my shift."

Eric turned and raced to the stairwell and pounded up two steps at a time. At the top of the stairs, he gasped for a breath and flung the door open. Judy sat alone in the waiting room with her head lowered.

"Judy?"

"Eric, I'm so glad you're here," she cried. "Pete. His heart stopped. The doctor said he might not make it this time. He has to Eric. He has to."

"What happened?"

"I don't know. That nice woman...Captain Bromstrom's wife, Jessie...brought some flowers and all of a sudden Pete stopped breathing. Why is this happening?"

God, if he only had the answer. He sat beside Judy and clutched her hand. Unable to find his voice he stared at the dingy walls in silence and prayed.

Doctor Mitchell emerged from the operating room at nine-thirty. Beads of sweat gleamed on his forehead.

"Mrs. Hallman."

Judy looked up at him with wet, hopeful eyes.

The doctor took a seat on the other side of her. "He's in grave condition. His heart stopped twice during surgery."

Tears streamed down Judy's cheeks. "He's going to make it, though, right?"

"We are doing everything possible—but he's in a coma."

"No." Judy threw her hands over her mouth.

Eric's hands balled into fists. *This was his fault.*

"We'll continue to monitor his heart. He'll be in recovery again for a few hours." The doctor paused for a second. "When you see him, talk to him and touch him. Hopefully, he'll wake up. That's all I can tell you right now. He's a fighter, Mrs. Hallman. He's young and strong. We need to stay positive."

"Thanks." Eric watched the doctor saunter to the elevator.

She clenched her purse against her chest. "Eric, you find the person who did this to my husband."

"I will. Come on. I'll walk you to the recovery room before I leave."

Judy looked at him. "What if Pete never wakes up?"

Again, Eric didn't have an answer. All he knew was he couldn't lose his partner and more than anything he wanted a drink.

* * *

After leaving the hospital, Eric had no trouble finding Jimmy Flame. Dressed in an oversized white shirt and white saggy pants, the kid looked like the *"Man from Glad"* with a tan.

Eric rolled down the windows and tapped the horn.

"Hey, man. I ain't gettin' in. Who knows where you'll dump me this time." Jimmy shook his head. "No way."

"I just want to talk to you. I promise. Hop in."

Jimmy gritted his yellow stained teeth and opened the passenger side door.

In front of the skeleton remains of a house, two of Jimmy's pals sat on the stoop with smirks on their faces.

"Wipe them grins off your faces," Jimmy yelled and slammed the car door. "What do you need from me now?"

Eric tossed a wrinkled one-hundred-dollar bill at him.

Jimmy's eyes lit. "What's this for?" He snatched the money and shoved the bill into his pants pocket.

"I'm feeling generous this morning."

"You generous?" Jimmy let out a laugh. "I don't buy it. Man, you're playing me."

Eric handed Jimmy a small piece of paper. "You can read, can't you?"

"Hell yes. What do you think I am? A dummy?"

"Read it to me."

"Is this a test or something?"

"You ask too many questions. Just read."

Jimmy seized the paper with discoloured fingers and squinted. "Black, '83 or '85 GMC van. Tinted windows, chrome grill. Bullet holes in the back door." He glanced up at Eric. "This ain't no grocery list. You lookin' for this?"

"Congratulations, you passed. Get that description out on the street. If you see that van, call me. You got it?"

Jimmy nodded. "Shit. You must want this bad. Real bad."

"I do." *More than you'll ever know.*

"Heard you got your old man's shooter last night. See you didn't need me after all. Hell, I didn't need to walk home a mile either," Jimmy grumbled as he got out of the car.

Eric glanced at his watch. "Stop whining. It wasn't a mile. Go work you're magic." He put the car in drive when Jimmy yelled at him.

"Stop."

What now? Eric slammed on the brakes.

"Hey, my Cuz here says he saw the van yesterday. Tell him Moe, tell him."

Eric looked at the kid with his hat on backwards. Not a day over fourteen he figured.

Moe pointed to the end of the block. "Those wheels were parked out front of The Watering Hole."

Eric straightened in the seat. "Did you see the driver?"

"Nope only the van—a real nasty piece of work with sweet, sweet wheels."

"Shouldn't you be in school?" Eric asked.

The kid's eyes darted to Jimmy. "Um...got the day off."

"Shit. Don't be givin' my man a hard time," Jimmy said.

Eric narrowed his eyes and glared at Moe. "You'd better be back in school next week. You understand?"

Moe nodded and stepped back from the car. "Nice wheels, man."

"Kid, don't even think about it."

Up the street, Eric parked in front of The Watering

Hole and got out. He could almost smell the liquor, taste the richness of it on his tongue. He stared at the hot pink neon open sign then peered through the dirty window.

Inside, a man sat at the scruffy bar slugging back a beer while country music hummed from the jukebox. Eric sat next to the man and looked at the bartender with a white towel slung over his one shoulder.

"What can I get ya?" the bartender asked.

"I'm looking for the driver of a black GMC van?"

"Look mister, this is a bar. Not the lost and found. Order a drink or get out."

"Eric pulled out his badge and slapped it on the counter. "Let's try this one more time. I'm looking for the person who parked a black GMC van out front yesterday. Did they come in here?"

"I heard you the first time. Don't need to be flashin' that damned thing around. You ever think to say you're a cop first?" The bartender filled a hazy glass quarter full of liquor and slid it across the bar to him. "On the house."

Eric stared at the golden liquid. Ice cubes crunched, and his throat ached. "What about the van?" He wrapped his fingers around the glass and gulped down the booze. *This is for Pete.*

"You're right. There was a van out front yesterday. The driver was a real looker. Seemed odd a pretty gal like that would be driving a piece of shit with nice wheels. She ordered a fancy drink, a lime daiquiri. I hadn't made one of those in years."

"Was she young? Old?"

"Mister, I'm sixty-nine. Everyone's young. Tall, blue eyes, long blonde hair, and very fine tanned legs. Oh, and she had a southern twang to her voice."

Eric's jaw dropped. The guy just described Amanda

Richmond.

CHAPTER SIXTEEN

L auren still couldn't believe Troy had been having an affair with Madelina. Talk about sleeping with the mob. What an idiot. How did he remove the murder weapon from the NYPD's evidence room? Did he have help from a cop inside? Before leaving the office, she'd made a quick phone call and confirmed the knife had mysteriously been "misplaced". The thought made her stomach flip-flop.

After Max left, Lauren decided to take his advice and not go to the police, at least not right away. She didn't want to do anything that might put her father's life in danger until she was sure Troy wasn't involved. She couldn't even tell her best friend what she'd learned about Troy.

"I feel so helpless." Lauren handed Amanda a glass of ice tea. "We're not getting anywhere with these lists."

Amanda patted her hand. "Eric will be here soon. Maybe he'll have some good news."

Lauren glanced at the empty coffee pot on the counter. "I just don't understand. Was he forced into the van? Did he really know the driver? Damn it, Amanda. If he's been kidnapped, why hasn't anyone called?"

"We can't think like that. Why don't we talk about something else until Eric gets here?"

Lauren sipped her orange juice. "You're right. With

everything going on, I haven't asked you about your vacation. I'm sorry."

Amanda slapped her hand on the table. "The hell with that. I want the down and dirty on you and Eric. Now come on girl, all the juicy details."

"There's not much to tell. Really. We met at the hospital after the accident."

"That's it? Is that all you can say? Good heavens. Haven't you noticed he looks even better than he did four years ago? Don't know how he could, but he does. Big hard muscles and that yummy firm ass."

Lauren couldn't help but giggle. "You're bad. And yes, I noticed. Is that all you can think about is a man's body?"

"Of course not." Amanda winked at her. "But it doesn't hurt. You're falling for him again."

"I do care about Eric probably more than I should."

"So, what's the problem? You're single, beautiful and brilliant. Be daring. Ask him out. Besides, you work too much."

She felt herself drifting into the same loneliness she'd felt in college. The eighteen-year-old who'd spent every waking hour in the law library and all day in class while life passed her by.

"I can't."

"Okay, now you're not making any sense."

Lauren stared out the patio doors. "Can you imagine loving a cop? You wake up and kiss him goodbye, knowing you may never see him again. All I can think about is Pete and his wife, Judy."

"I get it. You're scared. Sweetie, life is a risk and so is love."

"It didn't work the first time with Eric, why would it now?"

"Take a chance. Besides, aren't you getting sick of dating those dreary stiffs from the dating web site?"

"God, I hate it when you know me better than I know myself."

"That's what friends are for."

"I should take a quick shower before Eric gets here." Lauren turned and headed down the hall."

"At least think about it," Amanda yelled from the kitchen.

Lauren showered and then changed into a pair of jeans and a tomato red tank top. Through the kitchen window, she watched Amanda turn on her vixen charm. She swung her hips like a run-way model and teased the officer guarding the house to the fullest. Lauren swore the guy's eyes were going to pop out of his head.

If only she could be that gutsy when it came to men. Lauren shook her head then made a bagel with cream cheese and forced herself to eat. The knot in her stomach twisted tighter and tighter as each minute passed. She needed to find her father.

❋ ❋ ❋

By the time Eric left The Watering Hole, he'd turned away a second shot of liquor. Not because he didn't want the drink, but because he knew Amanda and Lauren were together.

The old bartender had described Amanda from her flamboyant style of clothing to her eye color.

He floored the Mustang down the highway and dialed his cell phone.

"Hello."

"Hey, it's Eric. Is Amanda still with you?"

"Yes. We finished the lists you wanted. She's in the

back yard playing with Lucy. Why?"

He paused for a moment not sure what to say next. Lauren was a smart woman and no matter what he said, she'd know something was wrong.

"I need to speak to the cop out front."

"God. Has something happened?"

He heard the panic in her voice. "No, I just need to talk to him."

In the background he heard footsteps, a door opened, and then Lauren said, "Detective Brennan wants to speak to you."

"Johnson here."

"Listen carefully. Don't say anything except yes or no. Understand?"

"Yes," the officer said.

"There's a woman with Lauren. Amanda Richmond."

"Yes, sir."

"Keep your eye on her until I get there. Lauren may be in danger."

✻ ✻ ✻

Eric opened the front door to Lauren's house, dashed down the hall to the kitchen and caught a glimpse of Lauren and Amanda sitting at the patio table. He slid the patio doors open and Lucy greeted him.

He picked up a tennis ball and tossed it. Lucy sped across the lawn.

"Lauren, can I talk to you, alone?"

"What's wrong? It's not my father, is it?"

"No. Come inside for a minute."

"I'll be right back, Amanda."

Lauren followed him into the kitchen. He closed the doors behind her.

"Listen to me—"

"You've been drinking. I can smell it on your breath."
She took a step back. Without warning, she spun around.

He grabbed her arm. "I don't have time for this. Now you're going to listen."

She twisted and freed herself from his grip. "I really believed you'd stopped drinking because that's what you told me. You're drunk."

"I'm not drunk. I had one drink. Yes, I made a mistake, but—"

"But nothing." She crossed her arms over her chest and narrowed her eyes."

"For Christ sakes, Lauren. I found a bartender who saw the driver of the van."

Her arms dropped to her sides. "What?"

"A bartender in Brooklyn. The guy described Amanda."

Lauren laughed and took a step back. "Now I know you're really drunk. Amanda and Troy were vacationing in the Bahamas. She wasn't even in New York."

He grasped both of her shoulders and looked her square in the eyes. "Are you sure?"

"As far as I know."

"Maybe they came back early, and you didn't know. Until we get to the bottom of this, be cautious. The bartender even said the woman ordered a lime daiquiri."

Lauren's hand froze on the patio door. "That's Amanda's favorite drink. This has to be a joke. She's my best friend. I'd trust her with my life, Eric."

"Come up with something to get her to leave. Please."

She slid open the patio door. "Amanda, I'm sorry to cut this short but Eric and I have to leave for a while. How about I call you at home later?"

"No problem." Amanda stood and slung her purse over her shoulder. "Is everything okay? You look upset."

"I'm fine. Just stressed. I'll call you?"

"Sure." She gave Lauren a hug and winked at Eric. "Take care of her."

"I will and thanks for your help. I'll walk you out."

Amanda got into her car and rolled down the window. "Why are you and Lauren acting so strange?"

"To tell you the truth we might have a lead into Stephen's disappearance."

Amanda's eyes lit up. "Really? God, I hope he's okay. Let me know if there's anything else I can do to help."

"Of course, and thanks." He stepped back from the vehicle. "You'd better get going. We'll be in touch."

Amanda's blue compact car sped down the driveway and disappeared out of sight. When he turned, Lauren was on the veranda with her purse in one hand, keys in the other.

"Where are you going?"

"Poughkeepsie." She marched down each step, and then unlocked the Mercedes.

Her body language told a story the way she was stiff, her mouth tense. She was pissed off.

"Not without me you're not."

He opened the passenger door and jumped in. "Look, I know you don't want to believe Amanda's involved. I can't say I'm convinced either. We have nothing else to go on. So, until we do, Amanda's a suspect."

"Now, my best friend's a suspect? How can she be a suspect when she wasn't in New York? Get real." She slammed the driver's door shut and rammed the key into the ignition. "You're wrong, Eric."

"I hope you're right. Because things aren't looking

good for Amanda."

* * *

In her heart, Lauren knew Eric was wrong. The bartender described Amanda to a tee right down to her hair style and eye color, but Lauren was positive Troy and Amanda were still in the Bahamas when the accident happened. Weren't they?

After learning about Troy's evidence tampering and his affair with Madelina, Lauren had her doubts. Why would Amanda want to hurt her, or her father? It didn't make sense. The bartender made a mistake. It wasn't Amanda. If it wasn't Amanda, then who? Should she tell Eric about Troy? God, she didn't know what to do. She didn't want to do anything to possibly put her father's life in danger.

In silence, Lauren sped down Route 9 and turned onto Main Street. While she drove past Coppola's Italian Restaurant, her mouth watered. She could almost taste the Shrimp Marinara soaked in garlic and spices and wished she'd ate something before rushing out of the house.

Eric scrubbed a hand over his face. "I haven't had the chance to tell you. Pete's in a coma. His heart stopped."

Her heart sank, and she kicked herself for not asking about Pete earlier. "I'm so sorry, Eric. Is he going to make it? "

"I hope so." He turned and looked out the side window.

Me too. She heard the pain in his voice. Frustration welled inside her. Lauren couldn't imagine what Judy was going through wondering if her husband was going to make it. "I really am sorry. We have to find the person who's doing this and find my father."

"Yeah, we do. And we will. Which reminds me. We didn't get a hit on that fingerprint from your patio door."

"For some reason, I'm not surprised."

On Nixon Street, she parked the car in the driveway of the colonial ranch style house, her home growing up after Jamie was killed. Lauren turned off the engine and got out. She still couldn't believe that Eric thought Amanda was involved.

Across the street, a dog howled. A teenager whizzed by on a skateboard. Wind rustled through the trees and a twig snapped.

She looked over her shoulder.

Eric scanned the shadows of the tall maples to the right of the house. "Come on."

After gathering the stack of newspapers from the front porch, Lauren handed Eric the key. When he unlocked the front door a rush of hot stale air greeted them.

"It's got to be a hundred degrees in here. Strange. Dad always has the central air on whether he's home or not. It was on when we stopped in after we were released from the hospital."

Eric pulled out his gun and pushed the door wide open. "Stay put until I check the house."

Lauren watched him disappear to the back of the house.

Minutes passed before he reappeared and shot her a reassuring smile. "Okay, all clear."

After she turned on the central air, Lauren checked the answering machine and listened to the messages. Five were from her, and one from Troy rambling on about the trial. The jerk had set her up to fail.

Eric rushed past her. "I'll check the garage."

She pulled back the curtains in the living room and

noticed the light layer of dust coating the coffee tables. Lauren had never seen a speck of dirt in the house before especially when her father had a cleaning woman come twice a week. In the kitchen, the coffeemaker was half full of cold coffee. She dumped the liquid down the drain and rinsed the pot. Even leaving coffee in the pot was uncharacteristic for her father.

Back in the living room, Lauren glanced at the black and white photographs of her and Jamie hanging on the wall above the fireplace. She stared at the last picture taken of Jamie a month before he died. He looked so cute with his chubby little face and enormous dimples. No one could possibly know how much she missed her brother. Her father's words whirled through her mind.

"You can't blame yourself for the rest of your life for something your mother did. You were only six-years-old. What else could you have done under the circumstances?"

Guilt hammered deep at her soul. *I wish I could have done more...I wish I could have saved Jamie.*

"All clear in the garage," Eric said.

Lauren drew a deep breath. "We have to find him." She heard a tinge of fear in her voice and she prayed they could find her father and soon.

"We will. Let's start looking."

"For what?"

"Anything that might give us a lead."

Lauren sat on the leather couch and opened the mail. Nothing out of the ordinary. The usual junk mail, the phone, and electric bill. The last envelope she opened was from the Chase Manhattan Bank. She examined the four-page statement when a cash withdrawal of twenty thousand dollars caught her eye. A chill bolted up her

Eric leaned on the back of the couch. "Find anything?"

"Maybe. A large withdrawal." She handed Eric the paper. "Check out the sixth."

He looked at the date. "Interesting. Where does he keep the rest of his bank statements?"

Lauren raised her head. "In a metal box in the top drawer of the desk in the den."

"I'll get them"

Eric returned with the long rectangular box and set it on the couch beside her.

Lauren retrieved August's statement and examined it. "Look, the same amount was withdrawn again on the sixth." She continued to study the previous six months. Her throat tightened. "They're identical. Do you think he was being blackmailed?" Worry plagued her stomach, knotting and gnawing. Maybe she should tell Eric what she'd learned about Gino Valdina and Troy.

Eric shrugged. "The withdrawals are suspicious. Any ideas on who might be trying to blackmail him?"

She opened her mouth to answer.

A deafening crack shook the room, like lightning hitting a tree only feet away.

The living room window imploded.

Lauren ducked and covered her head with her arms. Shards of glass fired across the room like missiles. "Eric!"

He dropped to the carpet and yanked her off the couch. "Crawl to the kitchen and stay there!"

Moving on her hands and knees, she headed toward the kitchen as another gunshot rang out. This time the bullet bore into the wall above her head with a hissing hollow thud.

A large glass jar flew through the opening where the

window once was and smashed on the floor in the middle of the room, setting the couch on fire. The sickening sweet smell of gasoline filled her nostrils.

Tires screeched outside.

Flames roared up the curtains and raced to the ceiling and spread to all four corners. Choking thick black filled the room.

She stopped and glanced over her shoulder. "No!"

"Get out of the house!"

Lauren inched her way through the smoke to the kitchen. Once there, she slid open the patio door and gulped in fresh air. Her lungs struggled for a breath.

He grabbed her arm and pulled her to her feet. "Come on. We have to get out of here."

Once safely outside, Eric bent over with his hands on his knees coughing, trying to catch his breath. Soot covered his face.

Sirens wailed. Someone had called the fire department. Thank, God.

Lauren covered her mouth and stared in shock. Bright orange flames shot out of the roof and engulfed the house.

Her childhood home was burning to the ground and there was nothing she could do to stop it.

CHAPTER SEVENTEEN

Three hours later, Lauren returned home mentally and physically exhausted. Her father's house was nothing more than a charred skeleton of wood and bricks by the time the fire department had arrived.

Bile crept up her throat. The acidic taste of smoke lingered on her tongue. "This is unbelievable. Everything's gone!" *Photographs of her and Jamie. Of her father. Things I can't replace.*

"I'm sorry about the house." Eric put his hand on her shoulder.

He reeked of smoke and so did she. Both were in dire need of a shower.

"The fire marshal confirmed it was a Molotov cocktail that started the fire made with gasoline and a kerosene wick."

Warning signals went off in her head. Suspicion flared. "I think Troy might be involved."

Eric stared at her. His brows furrowed. "Troy? Why would you think that?"

She sat at the kitchen table. "Max Richards came to see me. My father had asked him to look into an internal issue at the office." Lauren drew a long deep breath before continuing. "He has evidence that Gino paid Troy to make the knife used to kill Madelina disappear. Eric, the knife isn't in the NYPD's evidence room. I checked. It's gone."

A muscle in Eric's jaw twitched. "That son-of-a-bitch." His eyes narrowed. "I knew the bastard was up to something. Gut instinct. It's not that easy to get anything out of the evidence room. There's a paper trail. Sounds like an inside job. Someone helped him. It wouldn't surprise me if there are a couple of cops on Valdina's payroll. When I get my hands on Troy—"

"It gets worse." Her stomach knotted tighter. "Troy was sleeping with Gino's wife. That's why Gino killed Madelina. She shamed him, shamed the family."

He stood beside her with his hands clenched. "Christ. I'll have them both picked up. Troy and I need to have a little one-on-one time."

Lauren could just imagine what Eric would do to Troy if he got his hands on him. He'd beat him to a pulp.

Her palms dampened. "No. Wait, Eric. What if Troy is involved in my father's disappearance? We need to find my father first. Please."

He stared at her for a long moment as if weighing their options. "You're right. Believe me. Once we find your father, Valdina and Troy are going to be sharing a prison cell. They can go at it and kill each other."

"The two of them deserve nothing less. God, why haven't we heard anything yet? I'm worried sick. Did my father get into that van?"

"Let's hope not. We'll find your father. Half of the NYPD is out looking for him."

"I need to know he's okay."

"I know." He checked his watch. "Listen, how 'bout I whip up some supper. You need to eat. I bet you haven't eaten anything all day. Then I need to get out of these smelly clothes and go check on Pete."

Honestly, she couldn't remember when she'd last eaten. "I'll help you. I need to be doing something. The waiting is driving me crazy."

Eric rolled up his sleeves. "Nope. You're going to relax." He snatched her hand and escorted her to the living room. "Be a good girl and let me cook." He handed her a magazine.

Lauren curled up on the couch and smiled as he left the room. It felt good to get off her feet. It had been years since anyone had cooked for her. She missed those days. She'd missed Eric. Hard to believe he was in her kitchen putting together a meal for them. All that was missing was a glass of wine. Exactly what she needed to calm her nerves. The waiting was killing her.

Downstairs, she opened the door to the wine cellar. The heavy seal made a swooshing suction noise. Walls covered in mold-resistant redwood gleamed under the lights. Four long rows of racks each held one hundred bottles, categorized by region and type. She was proud of her collection, a hobby she'd started after moving in.

She decided on a bottle of Beringer Merlot. As she turned, a dark red stream of liquid on the slate floor coming from the next row caught her attention. She looked around the corner into the next row.

Her heart slammed against her chest. The bottle of Merlot in her hand smashed to the floor. "Oh, my God!"

Her legs froze. She gulped air as if she was drowning. An obscene pool of crimson outlined her father's body. Blood pooled around her feet and soaked through her canvas running shoes. Lauren screamed.

Footsteps pounded on the stairs.

Eric blurred by her. He knelt and bent over her father's body. "Shit." After checking for a pulse in her father's neck, he looked up at her. "He's still breathing."

❋ ❋ ❋

At St. Francis hospital, hours passed, and daylight slipped into darkness. As if in slow motion, Lauren watched doctors and nurses rush in and out of the ER, their voices trailing into whispers.

Eric sat in the waiting room next to her, held her hand, and fired question after question—like if she was okay, if she needed anything. His lips moved but she barely heard his voice.

She was numb. The shock of finding her father turned her into a zombie, stripped her of any emotion. Lauren squeezed her eyes shut and all she could see was the back of her father's head, the gaping hole the gunshot had left.

And blood. So much blood...

Lauren sat on the chair at the bottom of the stairs dressed in her pink flannel nightgown. Mommy's voice yelled in her head, "I hate you!" She covered her ears and watched the two policemen standing by the front door. They looked so sad.

Daddy fell on his knees and hugged Jamie, but Jamie was all limp like his ragged old teddy bear...

Nausea rolled through Lauren's stomach and inched its way up her throat. Had her father pleaded for his life like Jamie had? She swallowed hard and opened her eyes trying to force the visions and thoughts away. But the images wouldn't disappear. It was as if they were tattooed under her eyelids. They'd never go away. Just like the image of her brother tumbling down the stairs.

A female doctor dressed in blue scrubs exited the emergency room with a sober look on her face. Worry lines feathered the woman's forehead, her eyes weary and dull.

The doctor walked toward her.

Lauren stood. A lifetime of memories rushed at warp-speed through her mind. A sob erupted from the back of her throat and she knew her father was gone.

❈ ❈ ❈

Eric witnessed the anguish on Lauren's face as tears flowed freely down her cheeks. Her painful sobs filled the waiting room. As a nurse tried to comfort her, her body trembled. He wanted to wrap his arms around her, hold her, and tell her everything would be okay. He still loved her and the pain she was going through was breaking his heart. There was nothing he could do. At least not right now.

While hospital staff continued to console her, Eric made a quick phone call to the second-floor nursing station to check on Pete.

He was still in a coma. His condition unchanged. At least he hadn't suffered another heart attack. What if Pete never woke up? The thought kicked Eric in the gut, something he prayed he wouldn't have to deal with.

More questions plagued his thoughts and refused to let go. How did someone get into Lauren's house and kill her father with two officers posted outside? Something didn't smell right. Were they on Valdina's payroll? It sure seemed that way. Eric rubbed his chin. Another possibility popped into his mind. Maybe one of them was the precinct's mole who was feeding Valdina's crew information. It sure as hell would explain a lot, especially how Valdina's boys were long gone during the last few drug busts. Whoever shot Pete and killed Stephen wasn't going to get away with it. He would make sure of it.

His fists curled. The strong need to hit something or someone was overwhelming, and Troy Granger and Gino Valdina were at the top of the list.

CHAPTER
EIGHTEEN

At one in the morning, Lauren rubbed her stinging and swollen eyes. *This isn't a dream. Dad's gone.* She hadn't cried this much since the night Jamie died. Grief squeezed her chest. Her soul felt hollow and empty, another piece sliced away. Then the panic set in, confronted by the realization that her life would never be the same.

I'll never see him again.

Eric handed her a cup of tea. The lines at the corners of his eyes deepened. "I promise we'll find the person who killed your father."

"We have to." Her voice cracked. "I can't believe he's gone." With trembling hands, she took the mug. "Thank you for letting me stay here. I can't go back to my house right now."

"The crime scene guys said they'd be done in a couple hours." He sat next to her on the couch and put his arm around her shoulder. "There's no rush. You can stay here as long as you want. I really am sorry."

Me too. She rested her head against his chest and listened to the steady beat of his heart. The warmth of his body made her feel safe. If only she could have found her father sooner...

"I checked to see if Troy and Amanda were still in the Bahamas the night you were run off the road. They were. Airport video surveillance confirmed it."

Relief washed over her. She never believed her best friend had anything to do with the accident and now she knew for sure. "If Amanda wasn't at that bar, who would impersonate her and why?"

"Maybe Valdina paid someone to pretend to be Amanda. Why would he do that? I have no clue. We will get to the bottom of this." He rubbed her shoulder. "I'm also beginning to think the fire at your father's house might have been a diversion to keep us away from your house long enough for someone to kill your father."

"Why kill my father in *my* house, though? It doesn't make any sense. This seems more personal than a mob hit. Maybe I'm just too emotional to see clearly right now. "Nausea rumbled in her stomach and her voice choked with emotion. "I still think Troy is involved."

"So do I but I'm not sure how. I know he's in deep. I can feel it in my gut. I have a guy looking into his financial records to see if he was blackmailing your father. As far as Valdina is concerned, I'll talk to my captain and see if the organized crime boys can pick him up." He ran his hand up and down her back. "You might be right, though. What would the mob gain by killing your father anyway? Valdina would be on trial for the murder of his wife regardless. And when the news hits that Troy is on their payroll, shit is going to hit the fan. The media sharks are going to have a field day."

Lauren stared at the guitar leaning in the corner of the living room and sipped her tea. So much was going through her head. The trial. Making funeral arrangements. Finding her father's killer. Eric...

She sat up. "With everything going on I forgot to ask about Pete. How is he?"

"That's okay. You've been through a lot." Eric kissed the back of her hand. "He's the same. Still in a coma. He's got to make it."

There was no denying the worry in Eric's voice. Her thoughts shifted to Judy and how terrifying it must be not to know if your husband was ever going to wake up. There was a lifetime of sadness swirling around all of them right now. The thought made Lauren's heart ache even more. God, she missed her father.

"Do you want another tea?" He kept rubbing her back, massaging along her spine.

She set the empty mug on the coffee table and forced a smile. "No. Thanks. What I need more than anything is a hot bath." She looked down at her dirty tee-shirt stained with soot from the fire and realized neither of them had taken a minute to get cleaned up. "I really want to get out of these smelly clothes."

He stood. "Make yourself at home. I'll grab you something to wear and throw your clothes in the washing machine."

Lauren liked this side of him, the old Eric, the one who didn't drink. As much as she didn't want to admit it, she still loved him.

CHAPTER NINETEEN

In the bathroom Lauren lit a candle, surprised that Eric owned one. After getting undressed, she slid into the Jacuzzi tub. Warm water swirled and bubbled around her. The sweet mixture of gardenias and oranges filled her nostrils. She leaned her head back and closed her eyes.

The house she loved was gone. So was her father.

What if she'd found him sooner? Guilt ate away at her soul. Maybe he'd be still alive.

Something brushed across her elbow.

Her eyes flew open. She jolted upright. Water splashed over the edge of the tub onto the floor. "God, you scared me, Eric."

"Sorry. I thought you could use this." He handed her a glass of white wine. "Don't ask. I now owe the couple across the hall a bottle of wine."

"Thanks. You're right. I needed this." She grasped the glass and took a big sip.

His eyes twinkled and flickered in the candle light. "I was sitting in the living room thinking about how much I still care about you. I wanted you to know that." His gaze ran down the length of the tub as he ran his fingers through her hair. "You're so beautiful."

His words melted her heart and made her smile inside. He still cared about her. *I care about you too.*

"I don't feel too beautiful right now, though. Far from it." She set the wine glass on the side of the tub and slid back under the water and rested her head back. She closed her eyes again. His lips touched her cheek with such tenderness. Her heart swelled with familiar passion. Passion she hadn't felt for years. He was so close, she could feel the heat from his body. Her pulse leapt.

"Do you know what you do to me?" he whispered, his breath hot against her ear.

The sound of his low voice echoed in her head. She fought to keep her eyes closed.

He swiped the bangs from her forehead. His fingers stroked the side of her face, softly.

Her skin came alive at his touch and sent prickles of excitement through her. Lauren opened her eyes.

Eric sat on the edge of the tub and dipped his hand in the water then ran his hand up her arm and along the side of her neck. He kissed her forehead, slowly and thoughtfully. He bent down and ran his tongue in circles around one of her nipples. She shuddered.

The outline of his muscular shoulders strained against the fabric of his shirt. Light glimmered over his face. God, how she wanted to touch him.

Under the water, his hand trailed down outside of her leg as his lips caressed her throat. "Tell me."

Her mind told her to resist but her body refused. "I want you," she said, barely above a whisper.

His lips found hers and pressed harder with each kiss. His tongue sent tingles up and down her spine. He raised his mouth from hers and gazed into her eyes.

She had missed him more than he would ever know. Missed his smile. Missed his touch.

He held out his hand.

She grasped his hand and stood, her eyes never leaving his.

He kissed the palm of her hand and helped her out of the tub.

She fumbled to unbutton his shirt, her palms fiery hot as she slid the shirt off his shoulders. Her heart beat quickened. He dropped to his knees in front of her.

His hands skimmed up and down either side of her body to her thighs. Heat sizzled between her legs. Her throat tightened. He was driving her crazy.

His tongue made a path down and across her stomach then explored between her legs.

He stood and took her hands and encouraged her to explore.

She unbuttoned his jeans, unzipped them and tugged them to the floor. He stepped out of his pants and boxers. Her body trembled with anticipation. Lauren couldn't wait any longer. She pushed him back against the wall.

He grasped her legs and lifted her, easing himself inside her, his eyes intense with passion.

She wrapped her legs around him and hugged his body, rocking slowly then faster. Heat rippled under her skin and scorched her body. Her fingernails dug into his back as she tossed her head back and moaned. Hard waves rocked her body as she came. "Eric..."

He picked up the pace and plunged deeper and harder. Sweat slid between their bodies and kept the friction at a minimum. His breath quickened, and his legs trembled. He thrust one last time and exploded inside her.

They held each other, their legs intertwined before

Lauren unwrapped her legs from around his waist and stood. The lower half of her body felt like rubber.

Eric kissed her lips, and then her forehead. He scooped her up in his arms and carried her into the bedroom and gently placed her on the bed. He stared into her eyes.

And at that moment, Lauren felt the love he had for her, an understanding, an assurance that things would be different this time.

CHAPTER TWENTY

L auren stared out the car window and bit down on her bottom lip. "I can't believe he's dead. He was everything to me, Amanda."

"It's going to take some time. I know he loved you very much. I miss him too. The office isn't the same without him."

Unwanted memories came flooding back and threatened to choke her. "You don't understand." Lauren's throat was thick with emotion as she spoke.

"What do you mean?"

Her heart felt as if it would burst. She needed to tell someone. "He's all I had. Remember I told you I had a brother and he died of cancer when he was young?"

"Yes. That must have been horrible for you and your father."

"It wasn't the truth." Lauren took a deep breath. "My mother killed him on the night of my sixth birthday."

Amanda's mouth dropped open. "Oh, my God. I am so sorry."

"Jamie was only four. She was drunk when she pushed him down the stairs."

"What happened to your mother?"

Lauren played with her purse strap. "She spent twelve years locked up in a mental hospital. I haven't seen her since that night and I never want to. I haven't told anyone the truth until now. "

"Not even Eric?"

Lauren lowered her gaze. "No."

Amanda grabbed Lauren's hand and squeezed. "I'm glad you told me. I can't believe someone would do that to their own child."

Up the street, Lauren spotted the South Poughkeepsie Funeral Chapel. It looked more like a Georgian style home with its symmetrical shape and decorative front door with columns on both sides. The building was majestic. Her muscles tensed. Panic swelled in her chest, tight and suffocating.

"You can do this." Amanda steered the car into the parking lot and shut off the engine.

Lauren stared at the hearse parked at the side of the building. *This is real.* "I don't know if I can."

"We're doing it together, okay?" Amanda glanced at her watch. "It's only ten-fifteen. We still have forty-five minutes before the service begins."

"Thanks for all your help with the arrangements. I don't know what I would have done without you the past four days. My father cared a lot about you and so do I."

"That's what friends are for. It's going to be okay."

They got out of the car and walked to the front door of the funeral home. Tears welled in Lauren's eyes. She flinched and swallowed hard. The closer she got to the door, the more her skin prickled with heat. She turned to Amanda. "Could you see if I can have a few minutes with my father before the service begin?"

"Of course. I'll talk with the funeral director. Be back in a minute. Are you going to be okay?"

Lauren nodded. She leaned against the wall and fiddled with the zipper of her purse. She hated these places. The masked lemony antiseptic smell, the soft background music and the subdued decor. A cold shiver spiked up her spine.

Minutes later, Amanda returned.

"Mr. Hardy said to take you to the Garden Room."

"Okay." *I can do this.* Lauren kept her eyes lowered afraid to look up as they made their way to the room.

"I'll be right outside the door if you need me."

Lauren put her hand on the doorknob and took a long deep breath then opened the door and went inside.

He's dead.

The words echoed through her mind and beat at her heart like a fist, choking the air from her lungs. She looked at the open casket in front of the window and for a moment, the room spun and her heart lurched. Music drifted throughout the space and shivered through her like a ghost. The heavy sweet scent of flowers and the antiseptic smell of death churned together in a nauseating bouquet.

Lauren stepped closer.

There he was, dressed in the black double-breasted suit and the white shirt she had chosen for him. She reached and touched his hand. His skin was cold as marble, and reality slapped her hard. *He really is gone.*

His face looked unnatural, rigid, lightly tanned by the makeup and his lips were a shade too red to look real. She wanted to remember him her way, his warm smile and low raspy voice. A voice she would never hear again.

With a trembling hand, her fingers traced the etched leather design along the outside of the casket. Her heart ached with loneliness as tears streamed down her cheeks.

"I will always love you," she whispered.

Lauren glanced around the room filled with flowers. So many people had cared about him. He was known for his kindness and generosity. She walked to each arrangement, read each card, and inhaled each flower's scent then paused, remembering their dinner together at the Four Seasons on her birthday. She would carry the image of his smiling face alongside the image of Jamie for the rest of her life.

A tall brass vase with an overabundance of black lilies caught her attention. They looked out of place compared to the other arrangements of carnations, chrysanthemums and roses.

Lauren removed the card and read the handwriting on the back.

> *Lauren,*
> *Roses are red,*
> *Violets are blue,*
> *These flowers will die,*
> *And so will you.*

Fear swept through her. Her hands shook. "Amanda!"

The door burst open and Amanda came to an abrupt stop inside the room. "What's wrong?"

Lauren looked down at her hand, still clutching the card.

"What is it? Are you okay?"

"Find Eric."

"What's going on?"

"This." Her voice broke. "Look."

Amanda's eyebrows raised. She took the card and read it. Her face turned white. The card slipped through her fingers and fluttered to the floor.

* * *

In a designated 'quiet' room at the east end of the funeral home, Eric held Lauren's hand.

"The flowers were purchased at Twilight Flowers on Union Street. They weren't difficult to trace since most of the shops in Poughkeepsie don't carry black lilies. They have to be specially ordered." He shifted in the loveseat. "The owner said they were purchased by a woman with long blonde hair, a dark tan and a southern accent. She paid with cash."

Lauren's eyes widened. "Our mystery woman."

"Yeah. Flowers from the same shop were sent to Pete at the hospital a couple of days ago. Same type of threat but directed at him."

She rubbed her temples. "I don't understand what's going on. Why threaten, Pete? He has nothing to do with Valdina, Troy or the trial."

"I wish I knew. It's possible he may have been in the wrong place at the wrong time."

She let go of his hand and stood. "I've had enough. I can't take anymore. I can't even bury my father without being threatened by this lunatic. There are over three hundred people out there paying their respects to a wonderful man that I loved, and I have to hide in here." Tears gathered in the corners of her eyes. She was going to lose it any second.

Eric got up. "I know and I'm sorry." He put his arms around her and hugged her close. "I'm going to take you home to pack. I want you to go to your father's cabin. It's away from here and away from the city. You'll be safe." He kissed her cheek. "I'll meet you there in a couple of hours. I'm going to have a little chat with Troy and believe me—

I will get some answers."

CHAPTER TWENTY-ONE

A t the precinct, Eric sat across from Captain Bromstrom. Worry gnawed deep in his gut and he couldn't shake the sinking feeling something wasn't right.

Bromstrom slapped the cream-colored file folder closed. "I know Max Richards. He's one hell of a good private investigator. He used to be with the NYPD years back. If he says Troy Granger is on the mob's payroll, it's true." He scrubbed a hand over his face. "This whole damned situation is a mess. An internal investigation into the missing murder weapon is underway and Chief McClarin is furious. The media sharks are going to love this one."

Eric could imagine the media circus after the news hit that the assistant district attorney was on the take and evidence in the biggest mob trial in New York history had vanished. He shifted in the chair and glanced at the wall clock. Twenty past eleven. With any luck he'd be on his way to the cabin within the next half hour.

"I stopped by the courthouse. Judge Brookstein said Granger was a no-show this morning. I don't like not knowing where he is or what's he's up to." *The bastard is going to be answering to my fist when I get a hold of him.* "One of my informants is keeping an eye out for his Porsche."

"Good. Until we get the arrest warrant for Valdina and Granger, our hands are tied. Now what about Lauren Taylor? Is she somewhere safe?"

An uneasy feeling settled over Eric at the thought of Lauren being alone. "Stephen Taylor has a cabin in the Catskill's off Wurtsboro Mountain Road. Only a couple of people know about it. She should be there by now. I'll be heading up there as soon as I'm done here."

Bromstrom's eyes widened. "Something's bothering me. Do you think Robson and Johnson are working for Valdina?"

"It's bothering me too. I've known Robson since I joined the force twelve years ago. He's a good man. I'd trust him with my life. As far as Tom Johnson is concerned, I have no idea." Eric leaned back in the chair. "Perhaps one of Valdina's crew got to Johnson and offered him something he couldn't refuse because whoever killed Stephen Taylor had help getting into Lauren's house."

"Internal affairs are investigating to see if any laws were broken or if there was any professional misconduct on the part of either officer."

The phone rang.

The captain held up his hand. "One second, Brennan." He grabbed the phone. "Bromstrom...Yeah...Jesus Christ."

Eric sat up straight alarmed by the concern in the man's voice. He prayed the call wasn't about Pete. His stomach turned into a hard knot.

A long beat of silence, and then Bromstrom continued. "First Stephen Taylor, now this. Yeah, keep it from the media as long as you can. Thanks." He hung up the phone.

"What is it?"

"A couple uniforms from the 17th precinct found Granger's Porsche abandoned and completely stripped in Rose Hill. When they checked the vehicle, they found Troy stuffed in the trunk. He was shot in the back of the head—execution style."

Thank God, the call wasn't about Pete. Eric inhaled a silence deep breath and forced himself to relax. "So Valdina or one of his boys killed him. Guess the bastard was no longer useful to them."

"Looks that way. There's more. The organized crime unit lost track of Gino Valdina six hours ago. He's off the radar."

Eric didn't like what he was hearing. "Shit. He could be anywhere." Then every nerve in his body stood on end.

He jumped out of the chair. "What if he's going after Lauren?"

CHAPTER TWENTY-TWO

L auren woke confused. Her vision twisted and waved. She blinked and tried to focus. Candles lit the great room of her father's cabin. Shadows bent and deformed ripped up and down the walls.

God, the back of her head hurt. What happened? The last thing she remembered was unlocking the cabin... something walloped her on the head then everything went black.

She lifted her hand and realized they were bound with ropes to the arms of one of the chairs from the dining room. Her heart thumped against her chest.

Muffled voices filtered in from outside. A flash from the past weaved through her mind. Drenched in perspiration, feverishly she worked to free her hands but failed. The thick rope bite into her wrists. Blood slid between her fingers and dripped onto the carpet.

The voices grew louder. The front door handle turned.

A shiver rocketed up her spine.

The door flew open.

This can't be happening.

Lauren stared into the eyes of her father's killer.

"What's wrong, Lauren? Cat got your tongue?"

Cold pricking panic surged through her body. Tears welled in the corners of her eyes and froze.

"Now don't be rude girl, say hello to your mother," Madison said in a southern twang and slammed the door shut.

Oh, God! Her mother was the one impersonating Amanda. A wave of dizziness assaulted Lauren. Flashes of light and floating dark spots clouded her vision. The room spun. *Don't pass out.* She gulped for a breath and then another one.

Over two decades later, and Madison hadn't changed. At fifty-five she was still slim with long wavy blonde hair that hung down past her shoulders and she had the curves of a supermodel. She was dressed in a designer pink jogging suit and white tennis shoes and clutched a bottle of whiskey in her hand as if it was the last bottle of booze on earth. Even that hadn't changed.

Lauren yanked and twisted at the ropes around her wrists. The harder she worked to try to free herself, the deeper the ropes cut into her skin. "You killed my father. You, sick bitch."

Madison hovered over her for a moment then paused. She raised her hand and slapped her across the face. "Don't you talk to me like that. I'm your mother." She stabbed her finger in Lauren's face. "Where are your manners?"

Her cheek stung with fire. Lauren turned her face. "My manners disappeared the second you killed Jamie. And you killed my father. Why?"

"Oh, poor little, Lauren. Who put me in that nuthouse of a hospital for twelve years? If you and your father hadn't testified, I wouldn't have gone to that horrible place. This is your fault. You could have told the police the little bastard fell down the stairs. Stephen got what he deserved. Besides, he was going to cut me off financially. He owed me. I deserved that money after what you two did."

The mysterious twenty thousand-dollar monthly payments Lauren had discovered in her father's bank statements.

"The court put you where you belonged. Not my father. You killed your own son for God sakes. What kind of mother does that?" Tears streamed down Lauren's cheeks. "If it had been me. I wouldn't have given you a cent. You're insane."

Her mother's blue eyes narrowed and turned cold. A vicious smirk flashed across her tanned face. The same expression Lauren remembered the night Jamie died. Madison slapped her again, much harder than the first time.

I need to get free.

Lauren glanced around the room and focused on what she was going to do. She needed to find a way to cut the ropes around her wrists. It was her only chance. If she didn't try, her mother would kill her.

Madison grinned and held up the bottle of liquor. "You know it's taken me a long time to put this plan into action. As a matter of fact. Years. I'll tell you all about it after I pour a drink."

She sauntered to the bar like she was walking down a run-way and filled a glass with straight whiskey. The sight made Lauren gag. Afterward, her mother circled the leather couch in the middle of the room, and then sat across from Lauren.

"After I was released from that terrible hospital, I

started an affair with a wonderful man and I'm still seeing him, even though I remarried." Madison took a big gulp of her drink, and then grinned.

"Are you kidding me? I couldn't care less who you met. My father is dead. You killed him."

Madison waved her hand. "Oh, Lauren you're so dramatic. You always were."

After Jamie was born, Madison was unable to find work and began drinking heavily and it wasn't long before she fell into a deep depression. As depression and alcohol controlled her life, her fits of anger became more common, usually in the evenings, some more brutal than the others. Frequently Lauren was able to protect Jamie from her mother's fury, but not on the night of Lauren's birthday. She would never forget her mother's voice bellowing her dismay of giving up her life in the prime of her acting career for children she never wanted.

"You're the actress. Not me. Now untie these ropes."

Her mother's eyes narrowed, and then she laughed. Her cackle echoed throughout the room.

I have to get out of here. She'll kill me.

Lauren rocked back and forth in hopes of tipping over and breaking one of the chair's arms. Then maybe she'd be able to free her arms.

Madison dropped her drink, pounced off the couch and hurdled over the coffee table. She snatched a fistful of Lauren's hair and tugged. "You still can't behave, can you?"

Lauren kicked her mother in the shin with the heel of her foot. The blow forced Madison to let go of her hair and slammed her backward into the chair. She sat there for a long moment with dark eyes and a pathetic smirk on her face. She just stared at Lauren as if planning her next move.

What was Madison waiting for?

"Why did you shoot Pete Hallman? He has a wife. And now he's paralysed and in a coma because of you."

"No real reason." Madison shrugged. "He got in the way. Paralysed is better than dead I guess. I was going to finish him off that day at the hospital because he saw my face. But he went and had a heart attack. You know, being the wife of the almighty Captain Bromstrom does have its perks. I was able to get into his room. No questions asked."

"What? You're married to—"

"You heard me, Lauren." Her mother sneered. "You can call me Jesse if you'd like."

Lauren's stomach lurched. She wanted to throw up. What else had Madison done while planning her revenge?

The door to the cabin opened. The wind picked up and sent leaves scattering inside the cabin.

Lauren slowly turned her head. Her jaw dropped open. Gino Valdina.

Chills erupted over her skin. She was going to die.

"I got rid of her car. It's in the lake. No one will know what happened." He looked at Lauren then to Madison. "Is she giving you a hard time?"

Madison laughed again. "Not anymore." She got out of the chair, hugged Valdina, and then kissed him.

Panic flooded through Lauren's body. Wheels churned in her head remembering her mother's words. *"I began an affair..."*

Madison *was* Gino's goomatta—his mistress. The revelation sucked the air from Lauren's lungs. She gasped.

"Don't look so shocked," he said to Lauren. "Go get the plastic, Maddie. We don't want to leave any evidence."

Her mother nodded and headed down the hallway to the back of the house.

"Why are you doing this? Do you really think killing me will stop you from going to jail? I know Troy was having an affair with Madelina and when you found out, you killed your wife. Then you had Troy make sure the murder weapon disappeared. You and Troy set me up to fail."

"Smart girl. But you don't have any proof. My hands are clean. They always are. As for the assistant district attorney, I heard he's dead."

Lauren wasn't surprised to hear Troy was dead, but her heart ached for Amanda.

Valdina reached into his jacket pocket and took out a gun. He kept it held at his side and pointed at the floor.

Madison appeared in the great room with a roll of clear plastic bundled under her arm and a satisfied smile on her face. "Let's get this over with."

Her mother pushed the leather couch and coffee table out of the way, and then rolled out the plastic. When she was done, Valdina grabbed the back of the chair with both hands and dragged Lauren onto the plastic.

"Please don't do this. I'm begging you both."

Madison rolled her eyes. "Oh, Lauren. Shut up."

"Get back, Maddie. This is going to be messy."

Cold metal pressed against Lauren's temple.

She heard the trigger click when Valdina pulled it back. She squeezed her eyes shut and held her breath.

Lauren thought about her brother, her father, her dog. If she was dead, who would look after Lucy? Tears gathered in the corners of her eyes. She forced them back not wanting to give Madison the satisfaction of knowing how terrified she was. Then she thought about Eric, how much she loved him and wished she had the chance to tell him.

A car engine rumbled out front of the cabin.

"Who the hell is that?" Madison asked.

Lauren could spot the sound of that engine anywhere. *It was Eric.* She expelled the breath she was holding and opened her eyes.

Valdina lowered the gun and hurried to the window. "It's Brennan." His voice came out as an irritated growl. He looked at Lauren. "Don't you say a fuckin' word."

Madison stalked to the window and peered over Valdina's shoulder. "We'll have to get rid of him too."

"Yeah, we will. Now be quiet." He spun and pointed the gun at Lauren.

Madison walked over and stood in front of her.

The car engine shut off. A car door shut.

The great room was so quiet all Lauren heard was the soft hum of the ceiling fan. If they thought for one second, she was just going to let them kill Eric, they were wrong.

The door slowly opened.

Lauren spotted the tips of Eric's shoes before she saw the rest of him.

In slow motion, she looked up at her mother then with all her strength she raised both legs and kicked Madison in the thighs, knocking the chair to the floor and out of Valdina's line of fire.

"Eric! Watch out!"

The wooden chair broke into pieces. Lauren twisted and jerked her hands out of the ropes. She was free.

"You little bitch!" Her mother shrieked.

With her arms flailing in the air, Madison flew backward across the room and into the entertainment unit. Her head bounced back and hit the edge of one of the shelves with a loud crack. She slumped to the carpet.

Eric gripped his gun with both hands and aimed the weapon at Valdina. "Put down the gun. Now!"

Seconds passed and Valdina remained still. Then he pivoted and pointed his gun at Lauren.

Eric squeezed the trigger.

The bullet hit Valdina in the neck at the base of his skull. Blood and bone fragments rained down scarring the walls and furniture. The gun dropped out of his hand as his head slapped forward, and then back before his body folded into a lifeless heap onto the plastic.

Eric bent down and helped Lauren to her feet and hugged her. "You're safe now."

Over his shoulder, Lauren spotted her mother. Blood trailed down her neck and chest.

Madison's eyes popped open. She scrambled to her feet and let out a deafening high-pitched howl. She gritted her teeth and barrelled toward Eric like an all-star line-backer.

Lauren shoved Eric out of the way and dove for Valdina's gun. She snatched it up, aimed, and shot Madison between the eyes. "Go to hell where you belong."

The second Lauren saw her mother dead on the floor, a strange calm settled over her.

It was finally over.

Eric took the gun from her hand and placed it on the coffee table.

"This time *you* saved me." He put his arm around her and kissed her forehead. "I love you."

"I think we saved each other." *In more ways than one.* She leaned her head against his shoulder as they walked out of the cabin. "I love you too."

"Hey, I got a call from Judy on the way up here. Pete's

out of the coma. He has a long road ahead of him. At least now he has a chance—they have a chance."

Do we have a chance? She smiled. "That's great news. I can't wait to see Judy again."

Eric opened the car door and Lauren got into the Mustang.

As they drove, neither spoke for a long while.

His intense stare roamed over her face. "Lauren Taylor. Do you believe in fate?"

She held his hand not ever wanting to let go. "I do now."

ACKNOWLEDGEMENT

Much appreciation goes to Patricia Green at Room With Books for her insight and comments. Your friendship and support is priceless.

To my fans, readers and reviewers—thank you!

You rock!

Visit www.kimcresswell.ca and subscribe to Kim's Newsletter to keep up-to-date on exclusive content, upcoming releases, first-to-see book covers, contests, and more!